TABOR EVANS

LONGARM

AND THE RAILROAD TO HELL

JOVE BOOKS, NEW YORK

LONGARM AND THE RAILROAD TO HELL

A Jove Book / published by arrangement with
the author

PRINTING HISTORY
Jove edition / July 1991

ISBN: 0-515-10613-5

Jove Books are published by The Berkley Publishing Group,
200 Madison Avenue, New York, New York 10016.
The name "JOVE" and the "J" logo
are trademarks belonging to Jove Publications, Inc.

PRINTED IN THE UNITED STATES OF AMERICA

10 9 8 7 6 5 4 3 2 1

Chapter 1

"You're kidding, right?"

"Surely you don't think you're too good for routine work, Long?" Billy Vail's eyebrows lifted in the general direction of his balding, shiny dome, and he frowned. That and the fact that he'd chosen to call his best deputy by name instead of Longarm said that maybe the United States marshal for the Denver district wasn't having an extra good day today.

Deputy Marshal Custis Long sighed and crossed his legs. He borrowed time by pulling a cheroot out of his coat pocket and going through the rigmarole of getting it lit, then said, "You know I don't think anything of the sort. I'm just surprised a little. That's all. And, uh, there was this lady I was supposed to see this evening."

"Fine. Go right ahead, Long. I'm sure it's much more important that you get laid than that you get any work done," Billy said with heavy, and not particularly attractive, sarcasm in his tone of voice.

"Dammit, Billy, I'm sorry. All right? I didn't mean anything like that. An' you ought to know it by now. Hell, I'm sorry I opened my mouth."

Billy Vail looked like he was fixing to puff up and explode. His face became even redder than it usually was, and he leaned forward in his chair with his mouth half open. Then he clamped his jaw shut and subsided, leaning back in the office chair and swiveling around to face the window.

Not that the view out there was anything to treasure. The Federal Building on Denver's Colfax Avenue was surrounded by granite-walled office structures.

1

"Forget I said anything, okay?" It was an apology even if a grumpily delivered one. Longarm accepted it as such.

"Is there anything I can do, Boss?" Longarm offered.

"No," Billy said sharply. Then still without turning to face Longarm, he added, "My wife has been sick lately. Those damned useless doctors can't find anything wrong, so they can't do anything about it. I shouldn't be acting like this at the office. Sorry. It doesn't have anything to do with you or any of the rest of the men. And as for the rest of the men, for your information, everyone else happens to be busy at the moment. It's all perfectly routine work. Serving warrants and the like. You happen to be the best man available, and we do happen to need this prisoner picked up. If the job is beneath you . . ."

"Whoa, Billy," Longarm said quickly. "I already told you that it ain't. I'll be pleased to take the train down there an' pick this fella up for you. No problem. I can send a note to the—"

"No, there's no need for that," Billy interrupted. "You're right that the job is routine. Caswell is in custody already. He won't be going anywhere until it pleases us to go fetch him." The marshal swung his chair around so he was facing Longarm and tried to force a smile. The expression didn't come off all that successfully, but he was trying. "Look, it would be pushing it for you to try to make a southbound today anyway." That was a lie, but one that was offered with kindness and conciliation. There were at least two passenger trains scheduled south this afternoon and evening, and both Billy Vail and Custis Long knew it. "You can pick up the paperwork from Henry and take the morning southbound. There really isn't any hurry to get Caswell up here anyway. I'll tell the U.S. attorney's office to expect him sometime tomorrow evening. Hell, even if you left right now, it would be tomorrow before you could get him back here anyway. Right?" He smiled, a little more believably this time.

"If there's anything I can do, Billy . . ." The offer had nothing to do with a prisoner named Caswell who needed routine transportation from a local jail to federal custody.

"You might try crossing your fingers. Or, uh, praying if you're so inclined."

Longarm smiled. Billy Vail was a friend as well as a boss. "Whatever it takes, Billy. Right?"

"Right. Whatever it takes."

"And really, there's no reason why I can't start south this evening and—"

"Don't start that stuff with me, Longarm. Okay? Just pick up the papers from Henry and get on the first train south tomorrow. Marshal Kronnenburg has him in custody. You know Kronnenburg, don't you?"

Longarm nodded. He knew the man, although not well. Kronnenburg was the town marshal in Trinidad, and had been on the job there for only a matter of months. Longarm knew the county sheriff somewhat better. If he remembered correctly, the two shared jail facilities.

The prisoner, K. C. Caswell, was wanted on federal charges of mail theft and the murder of a mail guard.

K. C. Caswell, Longarm figured, was one truly dumb son of a bitch. According to what Billy'd just been explaining, Caswell hadn't been three days out of the Colorado State Prison in Canon City before he'd acquired a gun and used it to knock over a mail car on the Denver and Rio Grande running between Canon City and Pueblo. Nothing like a man getting right back to his chosen trade, Longarm supposed.

Caswell had been in the penitentiary there since the old rock pile was called the Colorado Territorial Prison. Served every day of a murder term that started sometime back in the '60s, and not a minute off for good behavior. If the idiot's performance since his release was any example, it was no wonder there had been no credit for good behavior.

Some folks, Longarm reflected, didn't find it real easy to learn simple lessons.

Dumb was what you could call that.

"If there's anything at *all* I can do, Billy . . ."

"I know, I know. If I can think of anything, Longarm, I'll tell you. And, uh, thanks for caring, huh?"

"Sure, Boss."

"Go on now. Enjoy yourself tonight and get an early start tomorrow."

"Thanks, Billy."

"Go on. Get out of here."

Longarm nodded. There wasn't a damn thing he could say or do here that would make his friend and employer feel the least bit better, so he stood and stretched, joints popping and tendons creaking, and turned to leave the marshal's office.

Deputy Marshal Custis Long was a tall man, well over six feet in height, and with a horseman's lean and narrow build. He had broad shoulders that filled out a tweed coat, and was a study in brown as he stood there in Billy Vail's office.

His hair and mustache were a rich brown. His tweed coat was a shade of brown, as were his corduroy trousers. He held a snuff-brown Stetson hat with a low crown and wide brim. A brown leather vest covered his torso, the sameness of its coloring accented by a gold watch chain that stretched across his flat belly from vest pocket to vest pocket. The chain looked innocent enough, but on one end of it was a bulbous Ingersol watch and on the other a brass-framed .41-caliber derringer that was capable of making large holes in solid flesh.

He also, and much more obviously, carried a double-action Colt Thunderer revolver canted at a crossdraw angle just to the left of his belt buckle. The .44-caliber Thunderer was capable of punching even larger holes than the derringer. And more of them.

It was said that the meek would inherit the earth. But then Custis Long had never had any burning desire to own the whole world. Meekness he would leave to others.

His face was deeply tanned by wind and weather, and was more rugged than classically handsome. Women, however, tended to make no complaint about his looks, so he wasn't going to complain about his appearance either.

He crossed to the door that led into the outer office and paused there, looking back at Billy Vail.

Billy had swung his chair toward the window again, but must have heard Longarm's footsteps pause.

"It's all right, Custis. Really," he said.

"Sure, Billy. If there's anything . . ."

"Nothing. Just . . . tell Henry that I don't want to be disturbed for a while this afternoon. All right?"

"Can do, Boss. And if you need me for anything . . ."

"I know where to find you. Check in here when you get back tomorrow, right? After you get Caswell bedded down in his cell. Maybe by then I'll have something more interesting for you to do."

"Right, Billy. I'll, uh, see you tomorrow."

Longarm tugged his hat on and let himself quietly out of Billy Vail's office. He wished Henry had warned him about this, though. Then maybe he wouldn't have been so fussy-particular about the boring assignment. Billy didn't need to be putting up with crabby deputies when he was worried about much more important things than prisoner transfers and warrants.

Longarm figured maybe he could make amends by making this prisoner transfer and every other dull and boring chore around the office go smooth as melted butter until Billy's problems were resolved and the marshal was back to being his normal cheerful self.

Yeah, he decided, that was exactly what he would do. And he would see to it that Billy's clerk Henry and all the other fellows did the same, by golly. That was the least they could do to give the marshal a helping hand when he needed them.

Chapter 2

Longarm opened one eye in response to the conductor's approach. He sat up straighter on the sooty upholstery of the railroad coach and lifted an eyebrow in inquiry.

"Just a few more minutes," the conductor told him. The question didn't even need to be asked aloud. But then probably everyone on the train was asking the same thing everywhere the harried man turned.

The Denver and Rio Grande southbound had been late getting out of Denver this morning, late again leaving Pueblo, had been held up in Walsenburg for more than an hour without explanation, and finally was approaching Trinidad, where extra pulling power would be attached by way of additional engines for the sharp climb over Raton Pass and on into New Mexico Territory.

Longarm nodded, satisfied now that they were finally arriving, and felt the train begin to slow as power was reduced. A few moments later he could hear the squeal of metal against metal as brakemen cranked the steel binders down a bit at a time. That meant they were within a mile or so of the Trinidad depot. And about time, too.

Not that Longarm had to be in any great hurry at this point. It was already too late to make the last scheduled northbound back toward Pueblo and, beyond it, Denver. Unless there was a special due through this evening, he would have to stay overnight in Trinidad and take his prisoner north tomorrow morning.

Longarm checked his watch to verify that there would at least still be time enough to get a wire off to Billy explaining the delay, and another to the U.S. attorney informing him that Caswell wouldn't be available for questioning until sometime tomorrow. It was all routine, if not exactly expected. No harm done.

Longarm stifled a yawn, settled his Stetson more comfortably atop his head, and reached into his pocket for a cheroot and match.

The brakes squealed louder, the shrill screeches sounding from one car after another, and the train slowed to a walking pace as the engineer eased hundreds of tons of moving machinery to a precise stopping point beside the Trinidad platform. It never ceased to amaze Longarm how a good engineer could judge his stop so nicely. It was a delicate balance of power, inertia, and braking force, and was a skill Longarm admired even if he did not fully understand it.

"Trinidad. Forty-minute layover in Trinidad. All out for Trinidad." The conductor came swinging back through the cars calling out his message. All around Longarm the other passengers began to gather up their belongings and crowd toward the doors even though the steps were not yet in place and the doors remained closed.

Longarm remained where he was. He was in no hurry now.

He let the others push and shove their way out of the coach, then in solitary comfort stood, stretched, and plucked a small luggage case off the overhead rack.

He was traveling light this trip. He'd fully expected to return to Denver with Caswell late tonight and have no need for any luggage, but long experience had told him not to count on that.

He'd settled for leaving behind most of his normal traveling gear—hadn't brought his customary McClellan saddle and bulkily scabbarded Winchester, for instance—but he knew better than to ever leave the city without at least a change of linen and box of cartridges. Now he was glad he'd gone to that small trouble.

His fellow passengers were already dispersing by the time Longarm stepped down onto the platform. Those who were leaving the train here were heading toward the street, most of them with wives or sweethearts or friends who had come to meet them. The passengers who would be continuing on through Raton and points beyond were mostly crowding and clawing at the coffee and sandwich counter nearby. Longarm was glad he didn't have to join that mob and elbow a path through people for the privilege of buying a meal that would undoubtedly taste like pasteboard and dishwater.

Instead he finished his smoke in comfort, then strolled over to the telegrapher's cubbyhole and wrote out messages first to Billy Vail and then to the U.S. attorney.

"These should be delivered before the close of business hours today, shouldn't they?"

"Yes, sir, no problem."

"Thanks." Longarm picked up his bag again and walked back out onto the platform. The additional engines were being coupled into place by now, and the passengers who would be continuing were already drifting back onto the coaches. Longarm turned away from the depot and walked toward town.

The jail and town marshal's office were four blocks down on the left, if he remembered correctly.

He considered the time, decided he probably should stop first and secure a room, and did so at the first small hotel he came to. It looked clean and quiet enough despite its proximity to the railroad station. And clean and quiet was all he would ask of it.

The room clerk accepted a government voucher for the room charges and exchanged it for the key to a second-story front. "Breakfast comes with the room, Marshal. We serve from five to eight."

"Thanks." Longarm didn't bother trying to educate the man about the differences between a U.S. marshal, who was basically an administrator confined by his duties inside a stuffy office, and a deputy, who was able to get out and do more interesting things in the line of duty. People just plain wanted to insist that anyone carrying a federal badge was a marshal. Trying to explain the difference, Longarm had concluded, was a losing proposition unless there was some point to it.

Besides, this particular assignment was no more interesting or exciting than sitting behind Billy's desk would have been, so today the differences seemed to be blurred all the more.

Longarm deposited his bag in a plain but entirely adequate room, pocketed his key, and went back outside.

He yawned—last night in the company of a young lady named Judith had been as late as it was enjoyable—and walked up the street to the local jail.

Trinidad Marshal Amos Kronnenburg was behind his desk. Kronnenburg looked up and smiled when he saw who the visitor was.

"Longarm." He sounded surprised, but pleased, too. "What are you doing here?"

"Working, Amos. Which I see you ain't."

Kronnenburg grinned and pulled open a desk drawer to receive the magazine he'd been reading. "What brings you to our fair town, Longarm?"

"They sent me to pick up Caswell off you. Billy didn't wire you to expect me?"

"First I've heard of it," the Trinidad marshal said.

Longarm figured Billy was so distracted with other worries that he must just have forgotten. Not that there was any harm done, of course. Henry had gotten the paperwork together, and Henry never forgot any damn thing. The paperwork would be correct right down to the last comma and chicken scratch.

It occurred to Longarm, though, that Amos Kronnenburg was frowning now.

"Dang train was late getting in, so I won't need Caswell until morning," Longarm said, helping himself to a seat in front of Amos's desk and offering the marshal a smoke. "You can keep him overnight for me if you don't mind. The Justice Department will pay you the day rate for his keep, same as usual." Longarm struck a match to apply first to Amos's smoke and then to his own. He leaned back in the chair again and said, "Is there something wrong, Amos? You look a mite upset."

"Wrong? Well, um . . ." Kronnenburg cleared his throat and peered at the coal that was glowing at the tip of his cigar. "You, uh . . . I sure wish I'd known you were coming down to claim that prisoner, Longarm."

"You haven't turned him loose or anything, have you?"

"No. No, of course not, Longarm. If anything I wish

we could keep him and hang him here. We have murder charges against him here, too, you know."

Actually Longarm hadn't known, but that was beside the point. Federal wants always took precedent over local charges unless the Justice Department decided specifically to handle things different.

"It's just . . ." Amos Kronnenburg cleared his throat again. "Dammit, Longarm, I didn't know there was a federal deputy coming, you see. And I've already turned Caswell over to a Texas Ranger to stand charges in Austin."

"The hell you say."

"I'm afraid so," Kronnenburg admitted. "The Ranger showed up here this morning with an extradition request in his pocket. He took it to Judge Frampton, and the judge issued a bench order honoring the transfer of custody. I gave Caswell to the Ranger not more than an hour ago. I believe Ranger Jepp said—"

"Jepp?" Longarm demanded. "Tom Jepp?"

"That's right. Tom Jepp. He's sergeant of Company F, Frontier Battalion, and—"

"Bull*shit*, he is," Longarm blurted out. "There's a bulletin out on *former* Sergeant Tom Jepp advising that the man disappeared from his Ranger barracks under strange circumstances an' should be considered armed and dangerous. I remember because my boss Billy Vail mentioned he used to know this Jepp way back when Billy was rangering and couldn't understand Jepp going bad this late in the game. Jepp is wanted on some petty little charge down in Texas, but to tell you the truth I think the Rangers are worried about him for some reason and just want to put a handle on him so they can figure out what he's up to before any mischief is done. You say Jepp showed up here with papers claiming Caswell? And your stupid damn judge turned Caswell over to him even though there are federal charges outstanding on him?"

"I . . . yes, dammit, that's exactly what I'm telling you, Longarm. Don't get mad at me. Judge Frampton issued an order telling me to hand the prisoner over to Jepp. What else was I supposed to do?"

Longarm opened his mouth to bark, thought better of it,

and clamped his jaw shut again. "Did you see the extradition papers yourself, Amos?"

Kronnenburg shook his head. "No need for me to see them. Jepp took them direct to Judge Frampton. All I saw was Jepp's credentials as a Ranger. And the order from the judge, of course."

"But why . . . ?" Longarm frowned and shook his head.

"If that train hasn't pulled out yet, Longarm, you can still ask Jepp about it. Or pick him up too if there's papers outstanding on him as well as Caswell," Kronnenburg suggested.

"Why in hell didn't you tell me that to begin with, Amos? Let's go."

Longarm was out of his seat and racing for the door even before he finished speaking.

Marshal Amos Kronnenburg came along behind at a considerably slower pace.

Chapter 3

"Aw, shit."

The train was already in motion, three powerful engines drawing it forward, overcoming the inertia of all that weight at a dead stop and slowly building momentum powerful enough to drag the cars over the steep and tortuous climb that was Raton Pass, separating Colorado and New Mexico.

Longarm stretched his legs and ran. The last cars were disappearing out of view behind the depot building now, but maybe he could still catch the damn thing.

He pounded down the center of the street, and almost collided with a light carriage as he dashed across the last cross street and into the final block.

He had to slow to avoid running into the gray horse that was pulling the carriage, swerved, and ran underneath the gray's nose.

There was a yelp of anger behind him as the gray reared, but he didn't have time to apologize at the moment.

He sprinted the last hundred yards, angled across the wagon park toward the platform, and saw the last car of the Denver and Rio Grande train disappear down the shining tracks.

"Damn it," he mumbled as he ran.

He didn't have a chance to catch the train now. The land was still flat here and the three hard-pulling engines were able to gain speed too damned quickly.

He ran on anyway, hoping that he might still be able to catch the back rail and pull himself aboard.

His boot heels thumped hollowly on the boards of the platform, and he sprang off it into the uncertain footing of the road ballast between the rails, almost fell, righted himself, and charged up the tracks after the damn train.

It was a hundred yards distant and moving at good speed now.

There was no way in hell he could catch up to it.

Reluctantly he slowed, then stopped and glared at the ass end of the train as it receded off toward the south.

A train whistle and puff of steam mocked his efforts.

Someone, a brakeman probably, was standing on the railed back platform of the last car. Longarm motioned angrily for the man to come back. The brakeman, now more than a quarter mile away and quickly increasing that distance, waved cheerfully back at the frustrated lawman.

"Shit," Longarm repeated.

He turned back toward the Trinidad station, and was greeted by grins and catcalls from the few people who had been on the platform there to witness his attempts to catch the train.

"She'll have t' find somebody else t' warm her bed tonight, honey," a rouged whore with hennaed hair teased. "But I'll be even better for you. Guaranteed."

Longarm scowled at the bawd, and went back out onto the street at a considerably slower pace than he'd just used getting there.

"Shit," he muttered again.

Amos Kronnenburg had stopped down the block, and was talking to the driver of the carriage whose horse Longarm had spooked. Amos had a hand on the gray's bit and was scratching its ear with his other hand.

The driver of the rig, Longarm saw, was a handsome woman of thirty or so with blond hair done in a severe style, a heavy gown buttoned high to the throat, and gloved hands. She might have been pretty, Longarm saw, if she hadn't been so tight-lipped and stuffy-looking. Her expression would turn cider into vinegar.

"Mrs. Beaulieu, may I present Deputy Marshal Custis Long. Longarm, Mrs. Catherine Beaulieu. Mrs. Clinton Beaulieu, that is." Amos acted like that name was supposed to mean something, and maybe around Trinidad it did. Longarm had never met the man and didn't particularly care to. Not if his choice in women ran to the kind that could curdle milk with a single glance.

13

Mrs. Beaulieu's nose lifted toward the sky and she sniffed loudly in response to the introduction. "I have no time to tarry, Marshal. Thanks to you I shall probably be late. You may deliver an appropriate apology this evening. Eight-thirty. Please be so good as to be prompt. Good day, Amos."

Without another look toward Longarm—which was probably a blessing at that—the haughty woman sniffed again and popped her driving whip over the gray's ears.

Amos Kronnenburg had to step lively to let go of the horse's bit and get out of the way of the wheels as the carriage lurched forward and rolled away at a spanking clip.

Kronnenburg looked at Longarm and shrugged. "I expect you'd best be there when she says, Longarm, and do some bowing and scraping to make the lady feel better. She, uh, she's old Clinton's third wife and figures to be his last. Heaven help us all when she takes over the coal diggings. Clinton accounts for half the jobs and more than half the money around here, and I'll tell you a natural truth. When Clinton says jump, I jump. I suspect we'll all be jumping pretty high when Miz Beaulieu takes charge."

Longarm frowned, then put Amos's petty worries out of mind. "Right now, Amos, we got more important things to think about. Like why a former Texas Ranger would be coming here pretending to have papers on a man wanted in Colorado. First thing, I want to talk to this judge of yours. Then I want you to tell me about the charges you have against Caswell here. I believe you mentioned something about a murder?" He took Kronnenburg by the elbow and drew the local man off toward the courthouse.

"No, Marshal, I'm sorry. The judge said he wasn't feeling well and would be leaving early this afternoon. Told me to cancel the rest of his hearings for today."

"What time would that have been?" Longarm injected, even though the court clerk had been addressing himself to Amos.

"Two, three o'clock, I suppose. No, now that's a lie. It was just before two because Judge Frampton had a two o'clock chambers hearing scheduled with Mr. Merrill and Mr. Watson on a probate matter. And he had me find them

14

and postpone that hearing. So it would've been before two. Not long before the hour, though. Counsel was already waiting outside the judge's chambers, and Mr. Watson is hardly ever early for anything."

"That would have been after he saw Ranger Jepp, I suppose," Longarm said.

"Oh, yes. The Ranger was in the judge's chambers through the lunch hour. The judge had me send up dinner for them while they talked. Then I had to draw up the order for him to sign and carry it over to Marshal Kronnenburg. The judge told me he was leaving when I got back from doing that."

Longarm grunted. "The judge was going home, you say?"

"Yes, sir, but please don't disturb him there. The judge is not a gentleman to take his duties lightly. He almost never asks for any delays on his own account. Why, I've seen him preside on the bench when he was so sick he'd be running a cold sweat and shaking with chills. If he's sick enough to leave he's awful sick. You shouldn't bother him, sir."

"Not unless it's necessary," Longarm said with a reassuring smile. He didn't add that he considered this damned well necessary.

He wanted to know why some pipsqueak local judge was suddenly deciding extradition questions that properly belonged between the sovereign State of Texas and the government of the United States of America. Unless the man was a real jerk he had to know better than that.

Longarm and Kronnenburg left the courthouse. The Trinidad marshal objected when Longarm said he wanted to visit the judge at home. Longarm's expression convinced him not to object too strenuously. The house, a large and lovely stone and timber dwelling with porches on both the first and second floors, was only a half dozen blocks away.

"I'm sorry, but Daddy isn't home," a girl of twelve or thirteen told them. "Have you asked for him at the courthouse? He should be there for another half hour, I think. Daddy is very prompt, you know."

Longarm smiled and thanked her. His expression flip-flopped into a frown once they turned away and the door was closed behind them.

"I don't think the child was lying, do you?" Longarm asked.

"What? Mary? Of course she wasn't lying. If you insist on seeing the judge we can go over to Dr. Collier's office, Longarm. That's where he must be. But I really don't think we should bother him—"

"Show me," Longarm said coldly.

Although suddenly he was getting the notion that they weren't going to find Judge Frampton at any doctor's office either.

Chapter 4

Longarm scowled into the bottom of the glass. A few drops of rye whiskey remained there. He raised the glass to his lips and upended it, savoring the taste. He would have enjoyed another, but he wasn't done working tonight. The railroad said there was a southbound freight due to leave Trinidad at 11:35. Longarm's badge promised him a place in the caboose when the train pulled out.

In the meantime he was welcome to sit here and stew.

Marshal Amos Kronnenburg was under no such constraints of duty. He helped himself to the bottle that Longarm had paid for and poured another shot.

"I can't understand this," Kronnenburg complained. "The judge has been such a pillar of the community. Then to just . . . take off like this."

"It's not against the law," Longarm reminded him. "A man can take off any time he pleases and go anywhere he wants."

"Something like this just isn't like him. He isn't a drinker, and I've never known him to fish or hunt or wander off prospecting. Never known him to do anything on the spur of the moment. He's always been a most orderly man."

Longarm grunted. By now it was obvious that there wasn't anyone in Trinidad who could—or at least would—give an explanation for the judge's odd behavior.

The man's disappearance was certainly voluntary. Ranger Tom Jepp—former Ranger, that is—was nowhere near when the judge told his clerk he was sick and would be going home. Longarm had to suspect that Jepp would have been able to explain it. But Jepp wasn't here any longer either.

Nor was K. C. Caswell, dammit.

Longarm had no reason to actively pursue Judge Frampton. But he damn well had jurisdiction to chase Caswell under federal warrants, and now Jepp too for interfering with Caswell's incarceration. That pair Longarm could and would go after. Quick as the railroad schedule allowed.

"You were gonna tell me what Caswell was arrested for here," Longarm reminded the local lawman. "A murder, I believe you said."

Kronnenburg drank off half his whiskey and refilled his glass quickly, as if he was afraid Longarm was going to return the bottle to the bartender soon. "That's right. Caswell murdered a half-crazy old sonuvabitch called the Major."

"Major?"

"That's all anybody knew him as. Like I said, he was a crazy old bastard. The town idiot, so to speak. Showed up years ago looking confused, and never looked anything different long as anybody here knew him. No doubt why he was like that, of course. He was scalped once."

"You're kidding me."

"No, I ain't. I swear it's so. The man was scalped, but lived through it."

"I've heard of such things, but I wouldn't call it usual."

"Well, it happened to the Major, let me tell you. This whole front part of his head"—Amos lifted up his hat and fingered his forelock to demonstrate the spot—"was all knobby red scars. And bald as a boiled egg. The hair never grew back. He had a scar on his throat where the Comanch' had cut his throat to kill him after they scalped him . . . or maybe before the scalping, he never said . . . but he sure musta been a hard man to kill. Called himself Major because that's what he was during the war. Confederate, of course. He was from Texas. After Caswell killed him and we cleaned out his room, we found papers saying he was a major in the Confederate Army and before that, maybe after too for all we know, a Texas Ranger."

Longarm frowned. Interesting coincidence, he figured, that this dead major was a former Ranger and so was Tom

18

Jepp. But likely it was no more than that. Just coincidence. He didn't interrupt Amos's storytelling.

"Musta been quite a man before the Comanch' scalped him and he went round the bend. When we knew him, though, he was just a harmless old coot. He'd do odd jobs. Panhandle a bit. Drink when he could get somebody to buy him one, but that wasn't often enough for him to be a proper drunk. We got enough town drunks without making the town idiot into one too." Kronnenburg smiled, but if he was expecting a smile from Longarm in return he was disappointed. It wasn't a subject that Longarm found particularly humorous.

"Poor old fella got a few dollars from someplace every month. Some sort of pension, I guess, though Barney over at the post office says the money didn't come in an official envelope and there wasn't a return address on the outside."

That wasn't common either, but Longarm supposed people could do things however they damn pleased. Including mailing pension money without a return address.

"Folks were kinda amused by him, and like I said, he was a harmless sort of codger. Never minded when somebody'd bring a visitor by to show off his scalping scars. People'd do that and usually slip him a dime or maybe bigger. Judge Frampton, now that I think on it, used to slip him money sometimes too. Dollar at a time at least."

Longarm leaned forward. Another interesting coincidence there. If that's what it was. Certainly Marshal Kronnenburg didn't see it as anything more.

"Anyhow the Major, he'd babble some but never made much sense of what he was saying. Too nuts to do much more than spit and babble when he'd try and tell a story and get himself excited. Other times, when he wasn't trying to spin a yarn, he could talk almost normal. To ask for a drink, say, or buy something at the store. But when he'd get worked up he couldn't string the words together, and folks would either laugh at him or else get disgusted and move away. When he was like that and trying to talk, you didn't wanta stand too close in front of him because the spit'd fly off his lips and drench your damn shirt if you

19

didn't move quick." Kronnenburg took a swallow of rye and filled his glass to the brim again.

"Wasn't but one thing the old fellow cared about, and that was a worn-out, useless old gun. Carried that damn gun with him every minute of his life. I expect that's what got him killed."

"How's that?" Longarm asked.

"Oh, it wasn't in no gunfight, I can tell you that. He never had any cartridges for the thing. I mean, I don't expect they even make them for an old crock like that no more. This gun, it wasn't even a brass cartridge model. You carry one of those newfangled double-action Colts, I see, but I'm sure you're old enough to remember the cap-and-ball Colts like everybody carried during the war."

"Of course."

"This thing the Major had, it was even older than them, if you can believe it. Damnedest old gun I ever saw. It was a Colt, all right, which I seen for myself when he showed it to me. But the stampings on the barrel claimed it wasn't made in Connecticut like every other Colt I ever heard of. It was made in New Jersey. And it was a funny-looking thing, not at all like a regular Colt revolver. No trigger guard on it. Instead, when you cocked the hammer there was this dinky little trigger would pop out of the grip. And no loading ram built onto the side like all the guns you and me might remember. If you'd want to load the thing . . . though to my mind it would take a damn fool to want to actually fire off an antique like that, crazy thing would be more apt to blow up in your hand than not . . . you'd have to stuff in the powder and ball however you could manage. Probably take it apart to get at it even. And that's if you could figure out what size ball it should take. It wasn't any .44 like the old army issue. Might have been a .36, but I'm not even sure about that. Could've been even smaller than a .36, although I'm no judge. For sure not a .44.

"Anyhow, old and useless as it was, it was still a pretty thing. Had engraving on the cylinder, and you could see where years and years ago there might've been some gold inlay set into the scrollwork, though if there was, all the gold was either worn away or else picked out and sold.

"Had ivory grips too. Carved real pretty. The ivory was yellowed and checked from being so old, but the carving was still awful pretty. One side had a raised carving showing an Indian with a lance chasing after a running buffalo. The other side showed a star surrounded by a bunch of banners and scrolls and stuff. You could see where there used to be words written on the banners, but I expect the Major'd dropped it or something because part of that was knocked off. The old gun had sure been a presentation piece once upon a time, though. It was still a handsome thing even now. Useless but handsome." Kronnenburg sighed and had another drink. "That SOB Caswell must have thought it was valuable or something, because that's the only thing he stole when he killed the Major."

"Oh?"

"Yeah. It was late at night, and the husband of the woman that runs the boardinghouse where the Major lived heard this commotion. Thought maybe the Major was dying, so he went up there and saw Caswell standing over the Major's bed with his hands wrapped around the old boy's throat. Strangling him, he was. The Major thumping and banging and trying to get free was what he'd heard. Caswell saw that he was discovered and there wasn't any use trying to be quiet no more, so he let go of the Major and whipped out a gun. Shot first into the Major's face, which gave the witness time enough to jump for the door frame. Shot again at the witness, then grabbed up the Major's old gun off the nightstand and ran for the window.

"The man, of course, he set up a howl to go along with the disturbance of the gunshots, and people started running. Caswell, he was on the roof of the wash shed built on the back of the boardinghouse. Damn fool put the Major's useless old gun into his holster and dropped his own good Colt so he could hang off the eaves and drop to the ground. I expect it's a good thing he made that mistake or maybe somebody would've got hurt that night. Other than the Major, I mean.

"Bunch of people were in the alley by then and surrounded him. He up and drew on them, but of course everybody could see that it was only the Major's gun he was holding

21

so they came ahead. Swarmed all over the son of a bitch, wrapped him up, and carried him to the jail for me to tuck away. Easiest arrest I've ever made." Kronnenburg chuckled and had another drink. "You know, it's a funny thing now that I reflect on it."

"What's that?"

"Why would that Ranger want that old gun of the Major's for evidence in a case all the way down to Austin?"

"There wasn't any case in Austin," Longarm reminded him. "And Jepp isn't a Ranger anymore either."

"Oh, yeah. I keep forgetting that." The Trinidad marshal shook his head and had another rye whiskey courtesy of Custis Long's bottle.

"Jepp wanted the gun as well as Caswell?" Longarm prodded.

"Sure did. Had it written right into the extradition order. I had t' turn over Caswell and the evidence with him. To wit, one engraved Colt revolver." Kronnenburg's features screwed themselves together in a caricature of a scowl. "That's odd, ain't it? I mean, that gun had t' do with our murder case against Caswell. But it couldn't have anything t' do with the charges against him down in Austin, could it?"

"There aren't any charges against him in Austin," Longarm patiently repeated.

"Oh." Kronnenburg laughed. He was becoming more than a little bit drunk by now. "Why d' I keep wantin' t' forget that?"

Longarm didn't feel much like laughing with the town marshal.

There was for damn sure more going on here than a simple prisoner transfer from point A to point B.

Longarm's problem was that he hadn't any idea in the world what the missing facts were.

He only knew that there seemed to be plenty of them.

And that *none* of them were making any sense right now.

"Marshal?" A young man wearing greasy overalls and a cloth cap was standing beside their table.

Kronnenburg blinked and seemed to have a little trouble focusing on the newcomer. "Yes, Pete?"

22

"I meant that one." Pete pointed at Longarm instead of his own town marshal.

"Yes, son?"

"The dispatcher sent me, Marshal. He said I'm to tell you there's a special has to be sent over Raton real quick. Something about a body being seen alongside the tracks, Marshal. I, uh, think he'd really like for you to be along. And he'll make sure you get on across to the New Mexico side afterward. If that's all right with you, sir. There's no sidings up there, so they'll have to delay the freight until the special checks back in, so if you want to go south soon it ought to be on this train."

"How soon is it leaving, son?"

"Quick as either you get there, Marshal, or else I come back and tell them you don't want to go."

"I'll have to stop at the hotel and grab my bag. Tell them I'm on my way."

"Yes, sir. Thank you, sir." The boy touched the front of his cap and hurried off into the night.

Longarm gave Marshal Amos Kronnenburg a quick hand-shake and left the bottle of rye in front of the local man, then hurried out in the wake of the messenger boy.

Chapter 5

Longarm sat behind the fold-down table at the side of the caboose, and held the coffee cup in his hand to keep the hot liquid from splashing all over him. At this slow pace the rail joints felt oddly sharper and bumpier than they did when the train was at speed, and he didn't want to put the cup down on the already insubstantial table surface.

This out-of-the-way corner inside the tiny caboose was the only place on the train that he'd found where he would not be in the way.

Not that there was so very much space to choose from anyway.

The special consisted of an engine, a coal tender, and the caboose. Nothing else.

Off duty brakemen and switchmen had been rounded up and issued lanterns, and now the railroadmen were hanging off both sides of the slowly moving special, trying to find the body that had been reported.

The message had come in the form of a wire sent from a coal mining camp a few miles south of Trinidad, and unfortunately was not specific about where the body was supposed to have been seen.

By the time the train reached the coal camp the telegrapher there had gone off duty, and no one awake seemed to know who had turned in the report or where the telegrapher could be found. The man was not in his own bed, and no one seemed willing to suggest what other bed he might be occupying.

The conductor of the special—actually the Trinidad-based section chief who was taking charge of the train but gratefully relinquishing to Longarm any responsibility if indeed a body was found—had to settle for ordering the engineer to creep forward at a walking pace with the lantern wicks trimmed as high as they would go.

At least Longarm had plenty of time to think while the conductor made his search.

This so simple case was not making sense.

Why had K. C. Caswell deliberately and in cold blood murdered a harmless old halfwit *after* Caswell was already discovered in the room strangling the old Major? Any normal thief should simply have fled once he was discovered. Or else shot first at the boardinghouse man, who at that point would obviously be more of a threat to him than the Major could have been.

Why did Ranger Tom Jepp abandon a distinguished career in Texas and show up here with false credentials to claim Caswell as his prisoner?

Come to think of it, Longarm realized, K. C. Caswell had been in custody in Trinidad for only two days. Barely long enough for word of the arrest and identification to have reached Denver.

Longarm heard about Jepp's flight from his own fellow Rangers *before K. C. Caswell was released from prison*.

Had Jepp deliberately turned his back on his career and headed this way specifically for the purpose of meeting Caswell here? Why?

And what was the attraction both of them seemed to have to an old and useless Colt revolver owned by a former Confederate major who also happened to be a former Texas Ranger?

It seemed too much to ask of coincidence that Caswell would idly have chosen to grab that gun and run with it, then thrown away a modern weapon but retained the old one while he was trying to get away from the Major's awakened neighbors. Especially when you topped that oddity off with the second one, that Tom Jepp had demanded that the gun be turned over to him as evidence in a court case that didn't exist.

The gun itself was worth virtually nothing, Longarm knew.

Trinidad Marshal Amos Kronnenburg knew nothing about

the New Jersey-made Colts, but Longarm had seen one now and then. Not often, of course. The things were rare, mostly because while that particular model had been the first practical, workable revolving-pistol design, the things simply weren't much good.

Not, at least, compared with a modern weapon. Even a Civil War–era cap-and-ball revolver was immeasurably better than those creaky old Paterson, New Jersey, guns.

A man could reload a Colt cap-and-ball while on horseback using flashpaper cartridges and the loading ram slung under the barrel.

A Paterson Colt had to be disassembled and its cylinder removed before it could be reloaded, and then the task was only easy if a special stand and tool were used.

The unprotected trigger mechanism was fragile and the mainsprings weak.

All in all, Longarm had been told, the guns were pitiful by any modern standard.

On the other hand, a generation or more ago the Paterson Colt had been head and shoulders above the single-shot, muzzle-loading horse pistols that were otherwise available, if only because the Paterson was capable of firing five times before it had to be reloaded.

Longarm had heard Billy Vail tell about a fight way back even before Billy's time when a company of Texas Rangers armed with those then-new Colt Revolving Pistols had run into a bunch of Comanches and killed thirty-odd Indians out of a war party of seventy or more. The Ranger company had been outnumbered but not outgunned by a tribe that had never faced repeating arms before, and the Rangers had owned the field when that one was done. Somewhere down along the Brazos, Longarm thought Billy had said. But then with Rangers everything seemed to be along the Brazos, which nowadays was tame and settled territory.

The Rangers—funny, Longarm reflected, how all of this seemed to be revolving around Texas Rangers all of a sudden—had cause to love the old guns back then.

But now?

Shee-it, now a man who owned a Paterson Colt might be able to sell the thing for fifty cents. If he was lucky enough

26

to find a sentimental sucker who had a yen for history and no need for practicality.

Somehow Longarm didn't think that a sentimental attachment to history was the key to this strange business here.

He took a sip of the scalding coffee and wondered where Judge Frampton fit into the picture. Assuming that he did, that is. There was still room for doubt on that one.

If Jepp's need to link up with Caswell had been great enough, well, it wasn't entirely unknown for a judge to allow himself to be persuaded to a course of action. In exchange, say, for a sufficiently large expression of gratitude. Preferably in cash.

But if that were so, why would the judge have disappeared within minutes after Jepp walked out of the courthouse?

It would take one hell of a sizable bribe to convince a respected jurist that he should violate federal statutes by turning Caswell over to Jepp. Even if he legitimately believed Tom Jepp to be a Ranger trying to extradite a felon.

Frampton had a connection to the gun too, Longarm recalled, however tenuous that connection was. It was Frampton who insured that Jepp would be given the gun as "evidence" by an unsuspecting and not particularly bright Amos Kronnenburg.

Then the next thing you know, the judge's family is left wondering where the hell Papa has gotten to.

Surely the judge wasn't yet another former Texas Ranger, was he? Maybe K. C. Caswell too?

Shit, maybe this whole thing was a plot by all the former Rangers in the Western Hemisphere. Maybe they were all gonna get together with their antique Paterson Colts and reclaim Texas as a separate and sovereign nation. Except that had been tried already, hadn't it? More or less?

Maybe, Longarm decided, Deputy Custis Long was more tired than he realized.

He was beginning to think maybe he was as crazy as that scalped old major had been.

He wondered if there was any point to crawling into the narrow bunk built against the opposite wall of the caboose and trying to catch a few winks while the railroadmen with their lanterns completed the search along the tracks.

He finished off the cup of coffee while it was still too hot to drink comfortably and slid out from behind the table. He was on his feet and heading toward the trainmen's bunk when someone shouted and the short special began to slow.

"Back up, Harry, I think I see 'im."

The railroaders' work for this night seemed to be done. Longarm's was just beginning.

Chapter 6

Railroadmen carrying lanterns surrounded the body, illuminating it and the red gravel slope it sprawled on.

The telegraph report had been no false alarm. The man seen beside the tracks here was as dead as he was ever going to get.

"What do you think, Marshal?" the conductor asked.

Longarm grunted and knelt beside the still figure. "I think the guy's dead," he ventured.

"It sure makes me feel better t' have a professional opinion about that," the conductor said dryly.

"Glad you're happy," Longarm told him.

The body was lying on its stomach, head pointing downhill. If it had slid another ten feet down the slope of the laboriously constructed railroad grade it would have dropped off into a gully and been lost to sight, might never have been discovered lying there.

Skid marks clearly visible in the gravel up the slope from the body showed that it had struck just a few feet out from the rails and slid the rest of the way. The skid marks were angled. The body obviously had been dumped off a moving train.

Longarm captured the scene in his memory first, and only then touched the dead flesh and turned the body over so he could see the features.

The body was cold and the night not particularly chilly. The man had been dead a good many hours.

It was hard to tell what the man's coloring would have been when he was alive, because blood had collected on the downhill side and now made his face unnaturally dark and mottled in the lantern light.

He was unshaven, with three or four days of growth stubbling his jowls. Longarm guessed his age to be somewhere in his fifties at the least. That too was hard to judge now. He had an untrimmed mustache and sightlessly staring dark eyes. Two teeth were missing on the left side of his mouth. The remaining teeth were yellowed and looked unhealthy.

He wore a cheap suit that showed little wear. Or had, at least, until the sliding fall shredded the brown cloth.

The dead man's hands, Longarm saw, were unscathed in the fall. He hadn't tried to stop himself from sliding on the hard gravel slope. And some scratches on his cheeks and forehead had not bled.

"He was dead before he was thrown off the train," Longarm said.

The conductor knelt beside the lawman and grunted, bending close to try to read the same sign that was telling Longarm so much.

Longarm pulled the man's coat open, exposing a tattered, shabby shirt that was much older than the suit.

A dark, reddish brown stain on the chest had seeped very little blood.

Longarm unbuttoned the shirt—there really was no need for that; it would have done no harm if he'd ripped it open, but the habit of tidiness prevented him from so much as thinking in those terms—and took a look at the dead man's chest beneath that small stain.

"Whoever killed him knew what he was doing," Longarm said. "See the puncture here?"

"That little thing? Looks like a pinprick."

"Deadly kinda pinprick then," Longarm said. "It's too small to've been a knife. Not even a stiletto. Ice pick, I'd say. Right into the heart."

"I always thought the heart was over to the side more," the conductor said.

"Nope. Damn near dead center. The killer knew that. Did a nice clean, quiet job of it. So there was others close by on that train that he didn't want to overhear the murder. One jab and the heart was ruined. Prob'ly put a hand over the fellow's mouth so he wouldn't cry out. A little thumping and squealing wouldn't be overheard above the sounds on the train, but a scream might've been. Or could be this dead man wouldn't of wanted to scream anyhow. I'm guessing that if we pull this fella's trousers down we'll find a bad scar high on the outside of his right thigh."

The conductor gave him a suspicious look. "Now how in hell, Marshal, would you be able t' see a thing like that?"

Longarm smiled. "Can't see it, of course. What I'm doing, mister, is guessing at who this fella is." The prison records on K. C. Caswell mentioned an old saber scar on that thigh as one of the convict's identifying features. And the cheap, prison-release sort of brown suit fit the likelihood that this was the prisoner Longarm had come south to collect.

"Let's find out." The conductor helpfully unbuttoned the dead man's trousers—he wasn't wearing a belt or tie or anything else that a prisoner might use to hang himself with—and two of the railroad boys set their lanterns down so they could help lift up on the corpse and haul the trousers down.

The dead, bloodless legs were startlingly pale. The saber scar stood out stark and livid against the pallor of the cold flesh.

"You know 'im?" the conductor asked.

Longarm shook his head. "Never saw him before, but I know who he was. He's the fella murdered the old Major in Trinidad and was turned over to that Texas Ranger today. Or yesterday, I suppose I'd have to say by now."

"Caswell," the conductor said.

"Uh huh. Marshal Kronnenburg will have to confirm that since he knows Caswell. But I think that's who we have here."

"But he was in custody by that Ranger."

Longarm didn't want to get into any long-winded explanations about Tom Jepp's status before the law. He let that go.

"Should I have my boys search for the Ranger's body too?" the conductor went on. "I mean, if the prisoner was killed, mightn't the Ranger have been too?"

"Possible," Longarm conceded.

Continuing the search in case Jepp had been killed along

with Caswell would be time-consuming. Men with lanterns would have to walk back at least as far as the trackside gully ran and look down into it. And they would have to search on toward Raton too. If indeed both Jepp and Caswell were killed, there was no way to guess which body might have been flung off the train first.

Longarm had a notion that there was no second body. After all, the judge from Trinidad was still unaccounted for, but at least on the surface of things he was not closely tied to this weird case. Longarm's immediate guess was that Tom Jepp was the murderer here and not another murder victim.

Still, guesswork was the same as damnfoolishness when it came to law work.

And Longarm had been known to be wrong about something once, maybe even twice, in his life before.

"I think we'd better look and make sure," he said.

"Ayuh. Hate t' do that. We can't allow any traffic south till this special clears the tracks. But I couldn't live with myself if I left a man lying out here to be chewed by varmints when we could've found him and brought him in for Christian burying. Worse if he was still alive somehow an' we walked away from him." The conductor stood.

"You heard it, boys," he said to his railroadmen. "Let's get to looking. Everybody with a lantern."

"We only have to search this same side of the tracks," Longarm suggested, "and no farther downhill than this gully runs. Anything north of that you'd already have spotted when we were looking for Caswell."

"How far south?" a tired switchman asked.

Longarm thought about that for a moment. "A half mile," he decided. "If you haven't found anything in that distance, we'll take this body back to Trinidad. Ask your county sheriff to make a better search come daybreak."

The conductor had promised earlier that they would take Longarm across to Raton if he wanted. But that wouldn't speed his progress by a single minute. There wouldn't be any more southbound traffic until the special was back in Trinidad anyway. And besides, Longarm wanted Amos Kronnenburg's verification that the body was indeed that of K. C. Caswell before Longarm went plunging off after Tom Jepp. Better, he thought, to go back and catch the first train that was released southbound.

"Let's get with it," the conductor ordered, and his workmen took up their lanterns and scattered once again. Longarm and the conductor hauled the body back up the slope and laid it out in the coal tender to await its final journey.

Chapter 7

"Just hold it," Longarm growled. He paused and added a belated "Please."

The conductor of the special may have sensed the tall deputy's frustration and been sympathetic. Or simply decided that he didn't want to risk Longarm's fury if anything was done to increase that sense of frustrated anger. After all, if the southbound freight was allowed to proceed without Long aboard, the conductor would still be there in Trinidad. And so would Longarm. Whatever the reason, the conductor nodded and said, "I won't let the train leave without you, Marshal."

"Thanks." Longarm sent a boy to find Amos Kronnenburg and rush him to the railroad depot, and another to rustle up a carry-out breakfast. He got two of the brakemen who had been part of the night-long search into Raton Pass to fetch a luggage cart and load the body onto it, but would not release the cold and rigid corpse to the local mortician yet. The undertaker had been at the station eagerly waiting to get on with his job when the special pulled in just as the dawn was breaking.

While he waited for Kronnenburg to be dragged out of bed, or whatever, Longarm went into the telegrapher's cubbyhole and started the long and laborious process of notifying every town and county lawman south of Trinidad that a murderer was headed their way.

"They're to look for a man named Tom Jepp, description to follow, who may be posing as a Texas Ranger," Longarm told the telegraph operator. "If Jepp is located he's to be detained but not charged. I'll be along quick as I can."

"Got it," the operator said. The man chewed on the ends

of his mustache and labored over the message form with a stub of lead pencil, adding words here and crossing out others there until he had something he and Longarm both agreed to.

"Gonna be expensive and take me a long time to get all this out," the telegrapher complained. "Who's gonna pay?"

Longarm gave the man a dirty look.

"I'll bill the county," the telegrapher said quickly. "That, uh, is where the murder taken place, I reckon."

"Fine," Longarm said curtly. "And mind now, you make sure everybody down the line gets that."

"How far?"

"Far as the rails run, dammit."

"Yes, sir." The telegrapher snatched up the message form and went to his key to begin transmitting.

By the time Longarm returned to the depot platform, Amos Kronnenburg was there. So was a growing crowd of onlookers. Apparently the sight of a murder victim was more interesting than whatever the early risers might find in the Trinidad cafes this morning.

"Is this K. C. Caswell?" Longarm asked Kronnenburg without bothering with the niceties of social convention.

"That's him, all right."

Longarm had been sure that it was, but he'd wanted the confirmation nailed down. Without that he was on mighty shaky jurisdictional ground for the pursuit of Tom Jepp and/or whoever else might have played a role in Caswell's murder.

"No doubts?"

"This is the man I arrested and who claimed to be K. C. Caswell and who I turned over to Ranger Jepp yesterday afternoon," Kronnenburg said formally. "You men are my witnesses," he added, pointing to several of the bystanders. Kronnenburg wasn't any great shakes as a lawman, but he obviously understood Longarm's needs here. "Whoever murdered this man done so in the state o' Colorado an' has since fled into New Mexico Territory. Deputy Long, I'm asking you to continue with this case."

"I accept," Longarm said, just as formal as Kronnenburg for this purpose.

35

Both men relaxed a bit, and Longarm edged out of the crowd, moving away from the body on the luggage cart and toward the freight that was being held until he boarded. "Thanks, Amos."

"Wish I could help you more," the Trinidad marshal said. "No question, though, that the dead man is your prisoner. Shoulda been, that is."

They reached the open door of the mail car, and Longarm made the long step up.

"One thing I notice," Kronnenburg said.

"Oh?"

"No wrist irons. And no sign that he'd been wearing any. When I turned him over to that Jepp, Caswell was put in irons."

Longarm grunted. That was a detail that he hadn't particularly noted, probably because he hadn't been there when the prisoner was extradited to Texas. So to speak. "You're right. No sign of chafing on his wrists and damn sure no cuffs on him now. Thanks, Amos."

"I'm new to this, but I'm trying."

"You're gonna do fine, Amos," Longarm said. Hell, it might even be true. He leaned down and shook the local man's hand, then said, "I almost forgot. I need you to give that telegraph operator a description of Tom Jepp so he can get it off with his warnings down the line. And would you send a wire to my people in Denver and tell them what's going on here? I forgot to do that myself."

"No problem, Longarm."

"I'll see you later, Amos."

"Luck to you, Longarm."

Longarm gave a high-sign to the man who had been the conductor on the special last night, but who now had reverted to his role as the railroad's section head for the Trinidad area, and up and down the length of the freight train lanterns began to swing and brakes released. The engineer sent a wake-up call to the town by way of his shrill whistle, and with a puff of smoke and a billow of steam four engines began to pull the cars south toward Raton.

Somewhere to the south, at least half a day ahead of Longarm thanks to the transportation delays, there was a murderer on the run. Tom Jepp, probably. Someone Custis Long had never heard of, quite possibly.

Who the murderer was and why he or she had bothered to knife K. C. Caswell to death were questions Longarm had no answers for.

But that, he figured, was a state of affairs that was subject to change in the real near future.

He nodded to the baggage clerk and the mail guard in the car he would be riding south, and crossed the swaying and jolting railroad car to join them at a small table.

"Mornin', gentlemen." His stomach reminded him that he hadn't ever gotten that breakfast he'd sent a boy for. Too damned late to do anything about that now, of course. He would just have to take his belt up a notch and wait for the next opportunity to come along. "Have a cigar?" he offered, and lit one for himself.

Chapter 8

"Fifteen minutes, Marshal. We drop two cars here and pick up whatever Raton has for us, drop off the extra engines, and roll on in fifteen minutes."

"Thanks." Longarm jumped down to the sooty gravel beside the freight siding and hurried toward the passenger depot a good hundred yards away.

The Raton marshal was there waiting for him. "I heard you were coming, Deputy. What can I do to help?"

"Give me Tom Jepp," Longarm said with a smile. "That'd be a good start."

"Wish I could, but I already checked with the railroad people here. Only two passengers got off at Raton last night. One was female, the other is a drummer who makes regular visits here. I took Jepp's description by the hotel this morning. The drummer says Jepp was on board the train with them last night and went on south. He doesn't remember seeing anyone with Jepp. Doesn't remember seeing Caswell at all."

Longarm grunted. The Raton marshal, though, was efficient. Those were the questions Longarm needed asked.

"I asked if he overheard Jepp talking to anybody, and he says he didn't. Wasn't sitting close to him. He did say that Jepp and some other fella—could have been Caswell, I suppose, but my man doesn't remember what this other man looked like—walked out onto the back platform at one point to have a smoke. But the two weren't together. Didn't sit together when they were inside the car, that is. And if they knew each other they weren't letting it show."

"Your drummer sounds like a good witness," Longarm observed.

"A traveling man, away from home, bored, got nothing better to do than look around and wait for time to pass, you know how that is. Damned helpful sometimes."

"Right."

"Wish I could do more for you."

"You can. I need a copy of the wires that've come down from Trinidad." Longarm himself didn't yet have a good description of Tom Jepp, and certainly not a written one. Besides, he could use those message forms in conjunction with his Caswell warrant papers to prove his jurisdiction if a question was ever raised about it. He smiled and added, "And I could damn sure use something to eat. Been a long time since supper last night."

"Don't worry. I'll get you taken care of."

Longarm found an outhouse while the Raton marshal was tending to everything else—some tasks a fella just can't delegate—and was comfortable and ready again by the time the train was ready to pull south.

Longarm grunted and growled, but there wasn't anything he could do about it. There was no stop scheduled at the Maxwell Ranch siding today, and the Denver and Rio Grande freight rolled past without slowing.

Just because the freight didn't stop now, it did not necessarily follow that the passenger train last night had breezed by too. Jepp could have left the train there, dammit, and Longarm would have no way to know it.

Even if Longarm had ordered the train conductor to stop, though, it would have done no good. There was no town there. No station or telegrapher or local law. Just a dry and dusty set of loading pens built next to a siding track. But it was a stopping point where any passenger could ask to be let off. Longarm wondered if Jepp could have known about that and used it to his advantage.

He could have, of course. But only if he'd thought about it ahead of time. A man put down afoot there would be in poor shape. He would have to have had a horse waiting. There just wasn't any way to know. Yet.

"Next stop is Springer, Marshal," the baggage clerk volunteered.

"Thanks."

"You gonna stay with us all the way?"

"If I have to." Longarm stood at the open car door and watched the monotonous grass plains rumble past his eyes. He lit a cheroot and leaned against the door frame.

Waiting wasn't one of his favorite pastimes.

"Half hour, Marshal," the conductor said. "Usually we'd be stopping here longer, but not today. We're running late and got to make up time if we can."

Longarm nodded and disembarked, hiking back toward the passenger station while the freight and car handlers did whatever it was they did. When the engine backed to the water tank he would know it was time to get back aboard or have to wait for the next southbound.

Unlike at Raton, in Springer there was no helpful and efficient local lawman waiting for him.

"He got your wires, Marshal," the telegraph operator assured him, "but I haven't seen him since." The operator turned to another man in the office and asked, "You know where Bert is?"

"Sure. He's out talking to Rick Knight."

"Again?" The telegrapher made a sour face and shook his head. Then he turned back to Longarm and explained. "Ol' Rick, he gets drunk now and then and beats up on his old woman. She gets pissed off and files assault charges against him. Then before anything ever comes before the justice o' the peace the two of them make up, and she drops the case. Bert gets mad about it, but there isn't anything much he can do except go over there once in a while an' ream Rick's ass for him. If he's with the Knights, Marshal, it could be after dark sometime before he gets back."

Longarm grunted. The sense of frustration was flooding over him again, and there just wasn't anything he could do about it. "Is there anybody else who could tell me about passengers who left the train here last night?"

The telegrapher kneaded his cheeks with one hand while he pondered the question. "Maybe. Just a second, Marshal."

He left his desk and disappeared inside the station offices. When he came back he had an old man with him. "This is Josephus Aurelius Smith, Marshal. He's our night porter. Joe says he was working last night when the passenger pulled in. Maybe he can help you."

Longarm gave the ancient, and improbable, Josephus a skeptical look, sighed, and posed his questions.

Yes, three people had left the train there last night. No, Josephus Aurelius Smith did not know them. Two were cowboys. Drunk, both of them. But they wouldn't share their bottle with Mr. Smith. They were very greedy and insensitive cowboys, Josephus Aurelius Smith thought. He hoped they both fell into water troughs and drowned. The other man was a very large man.

Longarm's interest quickened. Tom Jepp was tall.

The other man was nicely dressed. Very fat.

Longarm's face fell. Jepp damn sure wasn't fat.

The nicely dressed man gave Josephus a dime to carry his bag to the hotel.

Tom Jepp hadn't left the train in Springer either. He was somewhere further down the line.

But at least now Longarm knew.

"Thanks." He gave Josephus Aurelius Smith another dime for the old man's trouble and winked at the telegrapher. He might have talked to the operator more, but the man's telegraph key began to clatter. The line was being opened and a message sent.

Longarm ambled out onto the platform, and, bought a dry and tasteless cheese sandwich from a butcherboy, who with his basket of overpriced food items was waiting for the next passenger train. Then Longarm hurried back toward the southbound freight as the cars jolted into motion and the engine backed beneath the water tank.

Hissing steam and the gush of water filled his ears as he climbed back onto the mail car.

Off toward the station he could see someone wave. Longarm waved back to them and returned to the chair he'd been occupying all the way from Trinidad.

Where in *hell* had Tom Jepp gotten to?

Chapter 9

Longarm stood in the open doorway as the train slowed and lurched to a halt at Wagon Mound. The usual railroad workers were waiting there ready to handle freight. There was also a small knot of other men gathered close to the tracks.

"Are you Deputy Marshal Long?" one of the men called up to him.

"Yes, I am," Longarm admitted.

"Thank goodness."

Uh, oh. Longarm didn't much like the way the fellow said that. He jumped down to ground level. The men who'd been waiting for the train were already hurrying toward him.

"I'm Ron Bell, deputy to Sheriff Mark Thomas," one of them said with an extended hand.

"Most call me Longarm."

"I tried to catch you in Springer, Longarm, but the telegraph operator there said you'd already boarded the train. No harm done since you were already heading this way."

"What's up, Ron?"

"We got us a murder, Longarm. The body was spotted alongside the tracks earlier this afternoon." It was coming evening now, the sun fading behind the still-distant Sangre de Cristo mountain range.

"Popular sport lately," Longarm said dryly.

"Not so often around here, but I guess the exceptions are why you and me are getting rich feeding at the public trough, right?" Bell said with a smile.

Longarm laughed. A county deputy made even less money than a federal one. And Longarm so far had managed to avoid wealth in the line of duty.

42

"We don't know if this murder has anything to do with your case, Longarm, but we got your wires and know about the troubles up in Colorado last night. Figured we'd best bring you into it, just in case the two killings are connected."

"Good work, Ron."

"Aw, I'm not the one to thank, Longarm. I just strut around town with my chest puffed out and keep the star shiny in case there's any pretty girls watching. Sheriff Thomas is the one who left orders for you to be met and told about this. He's already gone down to where they found the body."

"You said this is along the railroad tracks again?"

"That's right. I already told the conductor. He'll let us off where he sees the crowd down the way. Almost down to the Fort Union siding, it is."

Longarm nodded. He knew Fort Union, of course. The post wasn't a normal army installation. It had no storybook walls or fortifications around it and looked more like a good-sized, well laid out town than a military post.

A long time back, Fort Union had been established to protect freight traffic on the Santa Fe Trail. It was placed inside the narrow V-angle where the old trail through Raton Pass and the dry Cimarron Cutoff came back together, and troops stationed there helped protect the wagon trains from marauding raiders coming off the plains or down from the mountains.

The frequently used wagon roads and later the coming of steel rails made Fort Union a logical supply point for other army posts in New Mexico and Arizona territories.

The place had grown so that now it was the army's largest and most important supply depot this side of the Mississippi. It was a huge, sprawling affair of warehouses, wagon parks, and blue-coated soldiers who worked with bale hooks, harness leather, and paperwork instead of sabers or rifles.

"Will the train be stopped here long?"

"They're hurrying it up," Bell assured him. "We'll be rolling again quick as they can manage."

Longarm stared down the tracks toward the south.

Tom Jepp was down there somewhere, damn him.

But where? And who had he killed this time?

Caswell's murderer almost had to be Jepp, Longarm had concluded.

But now this second body?

The judge from Trinidad came to mind. It wasn't impossible that the two could have known each other before Jepp showed up claiming to be a Ranger and demanding custody of Caswell.

If there was a connection there, well, it would take an almighty powerful reason to convince Frampton to abandon his family and his social standing and go off with a disgraced Texas Ranger and a wanted-again ex-convict.

But Longarm was beginning to think that damn near anything was possible in this case.

"If we have a few minutes, Ron, I'd better go send a wire to my boss back in Denver. I was supposed to've been back there long before now an' with a live prisoner in custody. He's bound to be wondering what's going on." Longarm didn't say anything about it, but he figured Billy Vail had enough worries on his plate right now without Custis Long contributing to them.

"This train won't leave without you, Longarm," Deputy Bell promised.

Chapter 10

There certainly was no problem trying to decide where the train should stop. There were at least two dozen people gathered at trackside, close to a mile marker warning the engineers that the Fort Union siding was nearby.

More than half the bystanders were wearing blue uniforms, so apparently word of the killing had spread to the military post. Longarm wondered if this particular stretch of track crossed army-owned property. It would make a difference about jurisdiction in the case if it did, because any crime committed on land owned by the federal government definitely belonged to Custis Long instead of Sheriff Mark Thomas.

"That's the sheriff in the gray hat there, Longarm," Deputy Bell volunteered as the train clanked to a halt. The engineer missed stopping beside the crowd by fifty yards or so, which wasn't bad considering he'd had no slow-down markers to judge by.

"Thanks, Ron." Longarm and Bell dropped off the caboose platform and hiked down the tracks to join the others. Bell performed the introductions between Longarm and Thomas.

The sheriff was a tall, thin man of forty or so. His bowed legs and suntanned features said he was no stranger to the outdoors, and there was a depth to his pale blue eyes that hinted he was no fool either.

"Pleased to meet you, Longarm," Thomas said as they shook hands. He turned and motioned toward the onlookers, and two straight-backed officers stepped forward and were introduced. One was a young second lieutenant who was officer of the day at Fort Union; the other was a lieutenant colonel named Harker.

"Is this matter under army jurisdiction?" Longarm asked Harker.

"It is not, sir. Post property does not extend to the railroad right of way. Lieutenant Young asked me to come with him, you see—I am post adjutant, by the way—because he is newly assigned to Fort Union and does not yet know many of our personnel. Our first thought was that the body might be that of one of our soldiers."

Longarm glanced past Harker's shoulder at the body sprawled in the gravel. The figure was that of a middle-aged man wearing a handsomely tailored suit. If the dead man was a soldier returning to post from leave, then the army had changed an awful lot while Longarm wasn't looking.

"Frankly, Deputy, I am glad now that I came," Harker continued. "I know this man. Knew him, I should say."

"Really?"

The colonel nodded. "Ralph and I went to school together. At the Academy." Harker shook his head sadly. "Terrible business, this. A sad end for a fine officer."

"I thought you said he wasn't army."

"Oh, I don't mean now. That is to say, he was not an officer in recent years. Ralph—Ralph Anthony Frazier is his full name if I remember correctly, and I am sure that I do—graduated with my class before the war. A Texan, Ralph was. He resigned his commission, you see, and took up arms with the Confederacy. Quite a waste, I always thought. Ralph was a true officer and gentleman. His choosing to serve the Southern forces was a waste of great ability. I've always thought that."

Longarm grunted. Ralph Anthony Frazier. The name meant nothing to him even if the man was known to this light colonel from Fort Union. Apparently the killing was unrelated to the murder of K. C. Caswell and the flight of Tom Jepp.

"Looks like this one is yours, Sheriff," Longarm said.

"I'm afraid so. I don't mind the work, but by now the killer is probably five counties away from here. It can be difficult crossing jurisdictions like I'll have to with this one," Thomas said.

"I know what you mean," Longarm sympathized.

Ron Bell had already gone over to rubberneck at the corpse. Longarm, Thomas, and the two army officers drifted in that direction too.

"Any idea what killed him?" Longarm asked idly.

"Single small stab wound to the left center chest," Thomas said. "A stiletto or smaller, I would say."

Longarm blinked. And frowned. "Shit."

"Pardon?"

"A stiletto or maybe an ice pick, would you say? One clean thrust into the heart?"

"That's right." The local sheriff was frowning now too.

"Dammit, Sheriff, that's the exact same kind of wound that killed my man Caswell up in Colorado."

Thomas fingered his chin. "I don't know about you, Longarm, but I'm no great believer in coincidence."

"Nor am I, Sheriff."

Longarm and Thomas knelt beside the corpse, and the sheriff pulled the dead man's shirt open. It was already unbuttoned from Thomas's inspection of the death wound.

"That's identical to what I saw on Caswell's body."

"There has to be a connection between the two."

"Yeah. But what. Any papers on him, Sheriff? Anything at all that might help?"

"I haven't gone through his pockets." Thomas began turning them inside out.

The dead man was no impoverished drifter, that was for sure. He was carrying a gold-cased watch on a diamond-studded pocket fob, more than two hundred dollars in currency plus some small change, a silk handkerchief, and a wallet, found in an inside coat pocket, that held more currency. In all he'd been traveling with nearly five hundred dollars on him.

"We can damn sure rule out robbery as a motive here," Longarm observed.

Thomas was thumbing through the small flaps and pockets of the wallet. "What did you say this fellow's name was, Colonel?"

"Frazier," Harker repeated. "Ralph Frazier, Class of '56."

"That's funny. There's some calling cards in here that say Raymond Albert Frampton."

"What!" Longarm blurted out.

"Here. See for yourself." Thomas pulled them out, a thin sheaf of perhaps half a dozen handsomely engraved cards, and handed one to Longarm.

"He certainly looks like Ralph," the colonel said skeptically. "Do you mind, gentlemen?"

Longarm and Thomas moved aside, and Lieutenant Colonel Harker knelt in their place beside the dead man. The officer was not squeamish, despite his current assignment to a supply post. He smoothed the dead man's hair down, rearranged the jaw, which had been hanging open, opened the dead eyes, and then took his time inspecting the slack face from one angle and then another.

"Gentlemen, I would almost be willing to swear an oath that this man was Ralph Frazier, not that . . . whoever you said. I mean, one does not forget a classmate. Ralph and I were on the fencing and equestrian teams together." A faint hint of smile briefly flickered and then died. "And we walked off demerits together many a time as well. No, gentlemen, I am quite sure that this man was Ralph Frazier, late of General Sibley's Mounted Volunteers."

"A man known as Frampton was a judge in Trinidad, Colorado," Longarm injected. "Until yesterday, that is. He disappeared just after he signed an extradition order transferring custody of my man Caswell to a man named Jepp who was representing himself as a Texas Ranger."

"This man is Ralph Frazier," Harker insisted.

"He could *also* be Raymond Frampton," Longarm observed.

"No. The Ralph I knew was an honorable man, Deputy. He would never do anything to dishonor his family name."

"Which could be reason enough to change his name?" Longarm suggested.

"Never," Harker insisted.

Sheriff Thomas was standing nearby frowning and pondering. "I think there's reason enough, Longarm, for you to take jurisdiction here."

48

"I agree with you, Sheriff. Though I'd appreciate all the help you can give me with it. If you don't mind."

"I'd be honored." The sheriff even sounded like he meant it. He definitely wasn't trying to pass the buck with the investigation, only to make sure it went as smoothly as possible. Deputy U.S. Marshal Long could cross boundaries and secure cooperation where a county sheriff from New Mexico Territory just wouldn't be welcome.

"You said a man named Jepp is involved somehow. That wouldn't be Tom Jepp, would it?"

"You know him?"

"Of course. He really is a Ranger, you know. We've worked together a number of times when fugitives thought they could evade the law by flitting back and forth between Texas and New Mexico."

Longarm smiled. "You must have an awful big county, Mark."

"Bigger than some states I could name. The point is, though, Tom Jepp really is a Ranger. I guess you didn't know that."

"Actually, Sheriff, Jepp used to be a Ranger. He got himself into some kinda trouble over there. Now the State of Texas wants to get hold of him too."

"No!" Thomas protested.

"Uh, huh. I don't know the details, but that's the word my boss got from his old Ranger pals."

"Tom was a fine officer."

Longarm frowned. "And so was Ralph Frazier a fine and respected judge until just yesterday. Or Raymond Frampton, if you'd rather. Do you get the impression, Mark, that there's stuff going on here that we don't know about?"

"Does seem likely, don't it."

"I'm commencing to think so. Colonel, do you have a telegraph wire at the fort?"

"Certainly."

"I'd like to use it, Colonel. Mark, I'd like for your people to take this body back to Wagon Mound and prepare it for shipment. I expect he should be sent back to Trinidad. As Frampton he had a family there. I'm sure they'll want him back for burying. But I don't know what in hell to tell those

49

poor people 'bout who he really was. Reckon I can worry about that later."

"I can take care of that, Longarm."

"It'd be a help too if you'd put out another want on Tom Jepp. Up and down the line. Urgent. You have his description, I suppose."

"Of course. I, uh, *thought* I knew the man pretty well."

"And, Colonel, I'll be wanting to get a statement from you attesting that the dead man is really this Lieutenant Ralph Frazier. Along with whatever else you can think of to tell me about him."

"I will assist you any way I can, Deputy." Harker frowned. "I think it would please Ralph if we were to refer to him as major, though, not lieutenant. I know he fought on the side of the enemies of our country, sir, but I have confidence that he did so with honor. I believe he should be entitled to the courtesy of his rank when he was with General Sibley. That association meant enough to Ralph that he was willing to resign his commission and abandon a promising career for it."

Longarm didn't offer any fuss. He supposed that army officers cared about things like that. "Yes, sir." He turned to Sheriff Thomas. "You and your people can clean things up here, Mark. I'm gonna go back to the fort with the colonel and get those wires off." He shook his head. "Somebody some-damn-where ought to have some thoughts about what's going on here."

"Will you be staying overnight at Union?" Thomas asked.

Longarm glanced toward the sky, trying to gauge the passage of time and remember details about train schedules that he really wasn't familiar with. "Prob'ly," he said.

"I'll do what I need to in town and get those messages off, then come down. We'll put our heads together and see if we can make two plus two equal half a dozen."

"All right. Colonel Harker, can I secure transportation to the post from you?"

"Certainly. At your convenience, sir."

"Then I expect we'd best get on with it, sir." Longarm shook Sheriff Thomas's hand and Ron Bell's, and followed Harker and his young lieutenant to a mule-drawn ambulance that had been converted for passenger use.

Harker motioned toward the knot of gawking enlisted men who had appeared out of nowhere to look at the dead man. The officer of the day immediately barked at the men, and the soldiers scattered.

The three men entered the ambulance in a militarily correct order of priority with Harker stepping in first, then Longarm, and finally Lieutenant Young bringing up the rear. Academy men were sticklers for little details like that, Longarm knew.

"Back to headquarters, Private," Harker ordered, and the driver snapped the team into motion and wheeled the bouncing rig toward the west.

Chapter 11

Fort Union had grown even bigger since the last time Longarm had seen it. The old buildings made of sod and rough logs were nearly all gone now, replaced by brick and native stone structures. The warehouses and corrals, barracks and mess halls, officers' quarters and office buildings stretched for half a mile or more. Off to the south Longarm could see the remains of the original fort, the old earthworks melting back into the ground now but still visible.

A huge garrison flag waved proudly over the massive parade ground that separated Officers' Country from the workaday portions of the huge supply depot. Men, mules, and wagons streamed in and out of the south side of the post. With all this bustling activity it was no wonder the railroad saw fit to lay a separate siding just for Fort Union.

"What's that?" Longarm asked, pointing beyond the fort to a ragged collection of log buildings in the distance.

"I wouldn't know, sir," Lieutenant Young said quickly. Longarm wasn't sure, but thought the young officer was blushing in spite of the denial.

Lieutenant Colonel Harker smiled a little, but didn't embarrass his lieutenant with a comment on the young man's stated lack of knowledge. "That, sir, is the thorn in my side."

"Sir?"

"They call it the Gates of Hell, which it most certainly is. Squatters, sir. Degenerates intent on fleecing poor enlisted men of their pay. Gamblers, prostitutes, even worse for all I know. It's also known as Loma Linda."

"I see," Longarm said. And so he did. There was no town close to Fort Union. Las Vegas to the south was probably the nearest settlement, and it was probably twenty miles or so distant. Too far, in any event, for a soldier with a few hours free to walk to it and have a drink, find a card game, or maybe get his ashes hauled. Most military posts had a Loma Linda or some equivalent. In fact, a good many thriving and now decent towns this side of the Mississippi had gotten their starts as a Gates of Hell close by the gates of an army post.

Longarm settled back in the hard ambulance seat and pulled out cheroots for himself and the two officers.

"I would rather you didn't smoke, Deputy," Harker said. "Sorry, but I lost a lung at Chancellorsville. I am afraid that cigar smoke has not agreed with me since."

Longarm returned the cheroots to his pocket.

The driver reached the main gate, and Lieutenant Colonel Harker responded snappily to the guard's salute. The ambulance stopped outside the post headquarters building, and Lieutenant Young jumped down to help Harker out. Unnecessarily in Longarm's opinion. But then maybe Harker and Young thought it was a necessary courtesy, and that was what counted here. Longarm was forced to get out of the rig too to make way for Harker. It would've been easier all around to think ahead about these things and have the guy get in last who would be getting out first. But that wasn't the army way of doing things.

"Lieutenant Young, you will be kind enough to secure visiting officers' quarters for Deputy Long, then escort him to the telegrapher and see that he is fully briefed as to dinner plans and anything else he requires."

"Yes, sir." The officer of the day came to rigid attention and saluted the adjutant.

"Deputy"— Harker was going on without pause— "you may call upon me directly for anything Lieutenant Young cannot provide. Also, sir, I shall begin immediately to prepare those statements you requested. They should be available to you by six o'clock this evening. My orderly will have them ready at your convenience thereafter."

"Thank you, Colonel. I appreciate your assistance."

"It is my duty, sir. Beyond that, it will be my pleasure to do anything in my power that will help find and convict the man responsible for Ralph's death. We were . . . good friends once, Deputy. Our later differences did not change that."

"I understand, Colonel. Thank you."

"Good day, sir." Harker snapped a salute to Longarm even though that was not militarily correct. It was, Longarm realized, an unspoken appeal from a down-deep personal level. Harker and Frazier had been classmates and buddies. Longarm nodded solemnly and touched the brim of his Stetson in return.

When he moved to climb back onto the ambulance he saw that Lieutenant Young was standing at attention waiting to assist him. And wasn't about to crawl into that rig until Longarm was aboard before him. It was easier on everybody just to go along with this petty shit. Longarm allowed himself to be assisted up the steps like a little old lady even though Harker was already marching stiffly up the walk to headquarters.

Young took Longarm first to the far end of Officers' Row where a small, stone duplex was available for visitors.

"You will be billeted here, sir," Young said formally. "This unit on the left is yours. Take any bedroom you like. If any bachelor transients show up before retreat, you may be asked to share the quarters but not the bedroom. The presence of young ladies would be, um, discouraged, sir. Wine and spirits will be available at the officers' mess, and package goods can be obtained from the commissary. I'll see to it, sir, that you have a transient chit there."

Longarm smiled at the shavetail, but knew better than to suggest he relax and loosen up. "Could I ask you something, Lieutenant?"

"Of course, sir."

"Just what rank is U.S. deputy supposed to equate to around here?"

"I . . . don't exactly know, sir." The young man puzzled over that one for a moment, then grinned. The change made him look even younger than before. But also more human. "About two grades higher than usual, I'd say, now that Lieutenant Colonel Harker wants full cooperation laid on for you. In fact, sir, if it would please you to have the

54

post band play you to sleep tonight, just say the word. I can arrange it for you."

Longarm laughed. "I reckon I can do without that, thanks. Just show me where I can find the groceries and that telegraph wire, and I'll be set."

"Yes, *sir*!" Young snapped. And grinned again. "Follow me, sir."

Chapter 12

It was a calculated risk, but one Longarm knew he was going to take. If Billy Vail chewed on him afterward, well, that was part of the risk.

Those wires requesting information were essential, dammit. Even more so, he felt now, than speed.

He would sit here at Fort Union and wait for the responses even if it meant losing another day in his pursuit of Tom Jepp.

Something very specific had to be going on here. Longarm's problem was that he had no clue as to what it might be. He was hoping that information the boys in Austin could give him might be the key that opened the lock.

Texas. This whole damn thing had a Texas connection.

Tom Jepp a Texas Ranger. Ralph Frazier, sometimes known as Raymond Frampton, a former officer in Sibley's Texas Mounted Volunteers. Hell, maybe K. C. Caswell with some Texas link too.

Longarm's telegraphed appeals to Ranger headquarters in Austin requested background information on all three of them.

Maybe, just maybe, there would be something in there that would allow Longarm to start making sense out of these murders.

Caswell fraudulently extradited and then murdered. Frampton, or Frazier, ordering that extradition, then abandoning his family and turning up a murder victim at the hand of the same man who killed Caswell.

And the murderer had to be Tom Jepp. Didn't he?

Longarm scowled at the ash on his cheroot, then reached over and tapped it into the pottery dish someone before him in the BOQ had used for an ashtray.

He pulled out his Ingersol and checked the time. Twenty to six. There was no point in walking over to headquarters before six for the statements Harker said would be ready then. Longarm had full confidence that those statements would be available at the stroke of six, not a minute later and probably no earlier either.

Longarm was hungry, but dinner wouldn't be served until seven.

In the meantime all he could do would be to fret and stew. And hope that some far-off clerk in Austin, Texas, would contribute to a manhunt in New Mexico.

It seemed a helluva way to conduct a chase.

Chapter 13

Dinner with the bachelor officers at Fort Union was a loudly gay affair. The stern faces and formal demeanor required when they were out where the enlisted men could see them were completely abandoned in the privacy of the officers' mess.

Longarm had no idea if the boisterous behavior was an every evening matter or if he had contributed to it by bringing a fresh face to the table.

Certainly the excitement was cranked up a notch by the fact that there was a gala slated for later in the evening. The hurriedly planned ball, he gathered, was being held with him as the guest of honor.

Any excuse to alleviate the boredom of an army post, he figured. Longarm expected he could put in a courtesy appearance and then go back to his quarters and read through the reports Lieutenant Colonel Harker'd had his clerk write up.

"Half an hour," Lieutenant Young told him. "We'll change and meet you there."

"Right," Longarm promised.

The officers streamed out of the mess, but Longarm lingered behind. He had no better clothes to change into, and half an hour wouldn't be time enough for him to get into the reports. He settled for staying where he was and having another drink. Officers at Fort Union, he'd discovered, had a bar that was stocked with quality as well as quantity. The rye he was given there was as good as ever he'd tasted. He had a glass and then another and smoked a cheroot. By that time he could hear the officers returning to the building and tramping upstairs to the big room that served for parties, plays, and occasional lectures.

Longarm ambled out into the hallway. And stopped short.

The caterpillar had gone and turned into a butterfly in just the past half hour.

Officers who not long ago had been weary and drab in their dark blue blouses now were resplendent in gold braid and bright brass. The dress uniforms were bright with color, and made even more fancy with brilliant sashes and gleaming swords. The shakos the men carried were gaudy with plumes in practically any color you cared to name.

Even more interesting, the women of the post now appeared on their husbands' arms or trailing shyly behind their parents.

There were more families at the post than Longarm would've thought. The men outnumbered the women by five to one, but even so there were gowns and lace aplenty.

Lieutenant Young sidled over to act as Longarm's protocol advisor. "You stay here till everybody is upstairs," he said. "Then you go up and pass through the receiving line. The post commander and his lady will be there." The lieutenant made that sound like one helluva honor. And maybe it was.

Longarm smiled a little to himself and patiently waited so the army boys could amuse themselves with him as their excuse.

"Yes, sir, I agree. Yes, sir, if I see the senator again I'll be sure an' mention your views on the subject." Longarm wasn't sure, but he suspected his eyes were starting to glaze over. The colonel had mentioned Senator Morley, and Longarm had made the mistake of commenting that he'd met the man once and escorted him around Denver. The colonel hadn't let up talking about the need for military appropriations since.

All around there were people dancing waltzes and reels and having themselves a fine old time.

Longarm was finding the evening somewhat less enjoyable than they seemed to.

"Marshal?"

"Miss?" The girl who was standing in front of him was small and chunky. She had a face whose features didn't quite match, like one side was taken from a slightly different-shaped mold than the other. He looked again and saw that her eyes weren't quite the same color either. One was definitely blue and the other was more a shade of gray. He'd never seen her before and had no idea who she was.

"I believe this is the dance you promised me, sir," she prompted. "Will you excuse us, Colonel, while I hold the gentleman to his word?"

"But of course, my dear." The post commander bowed, his dress sword rattling, and smiled as Longarm led the young woman into the middle of the dance floor where they wouldn't be on display from the bachelor line that rimmed the walls.

"My apologies," Longarm said, "for forgetting my promise."

The girl laughed and stepped into his arms and into the movements of the dance.

"You'd best be prepared to step lively," Longarm warned her. "I'm well known for stomping the feet of young ladies who tell lies."

"My name is Lenore Crane, Marshal. And I thought you looked bored quite to tears. If I was wrong, sir, I release you from the promise I know you would have made if only we'd met earlier. Would you rather go back and talk with the colonel?"

"Y'know," he said with a grin, "I don't generally dance much. But I can't think of a thing I'd rather be doing right now than dancing with you."

"I should warn you, sir."

"Yes?"

"My father is post physician."

"Funny, I didn't know that would be considered a warning."

"Around here it is. Daddy is all wrapped up in army politics. He's brownnosed half the general officers between here and Washington and *all* of them between here and St. Louis." She made a face. Lenore Crane was a homely girl, really, but there was something cute and appealing about her when she did that.

They swirled in time with the music. Longarm wasn't all that much a student of the dance, especially not this kind, and he wasn't sure just which of them was doing the leading most of the time. Still and all, between them they were getting the job more or less done.

"All the young officers here, you see, are frightened half to death of Daddy. And all the truly interesting ones are married anyway." She made that face again, then grinned. "Faithful too, darn them."

"Sad," Longarm sympathized.

"I certainly think so." She shrugged. "You would think that even an ugly girl like me could get herself laid once in a while on a post full of men."

Longarm missed a step and lurched. Lenore covered for him nicely. Almost like she'd been expecting it beforehand.

"The real problem"—she went on just like nothing had happened— "is that we had a terrible scandal last winter. All the young gentlemen had been enjoying the favors of a major's daughter."

"Quite a scandal," Longarm agreed.

"Oh, that was all right. The scandalous part was when they discovered she was sleeping with enlisted men too."

"I see." Sort of.

"Naturally she is gone now, and her father's career is ruined. Gwennie was my only real friend here too." The girl sighed again. "Worse, now all the young men are taking their urges over to Loma Linda and paying for it. Now I ask you, Marshal, is that the most truly unfair thing you've ever heard? Of course it is."

He stopped dancing in the middle of a step and looked at her. She smiled serenely back at him.

Longarm laughed and resumed the dance. "Really, Miss Crane, you should learn to come right out and say what you think."

"Oh, a proper young lady couldn't possibly do that."

"No, I suppose not."

The music ended. Longarm let go of Lenore and joined the others in clapping for the efforts of the band.

Lenore came closer and went up on tiptoes to speak into his ear. "I think I feel a headache coming on. Will you be retiring to your quarters? In fifteen minutes, say?"

"It has been an awfully tiring day."

"Thank you for the dance, Marshal. It's been very nice meeting you," she said loud enough for the other nearby couples to overhear. She stepped back and offered her gloved hand palm down for him to bow over. "Good evening, sir."

She twirled around and disappeared into the crowd, leaving Longarm alone in the middle of the dance floor.

He wondered if she really meant all that. Or if she'd just been creating a playful diversion from the boredom of strait-laced post life.

He wasn't honestly sure.

The music resumed and Longarm made his way through the dancers. The talkative colonel was over to his left, so he promptly turned right in the direction of the punch bowl.

"There you are, Marshal."

"Were you looking for me, Lieutenant?"

"Sort of. Lieutenant Colonel Harker wanted me to tell you, sir, that there is a civilian employee on post who knew Major Frazier during the war. In case you wanted to learn more about him, sir."

"Really? Now why would he think I wanted that?"

"Because of those messages you sent to Texas, sir, asking for background information about Mr. Jepp and Mr. Caswell."

"Sounds like it's a good thing there wasn't anything confidential in those wires."

"Yes, sir," Young agreed with a grin. Hell, these people weren't even apologetic about their snooping.

"How did this civilian know the major?"

"He was a trooper in the Mounted Volunteers, sir. But he took the oath again afterward, sir, and his citizenship has been restored. We have the paperwork here on all our former Rebels. Lieutenant Colonel Harker went to the trouble of looking through the records for you this evening just in case you would want to speak to anyone about the major."

"Please thank the colonel for me, Lieutenant, and tell him

I'll call on him tomorrow. In the meantime, I'm pretty tired. I think I'll pull it in for the evening."

"Yes, sir. Don't forget to pay your respects to the post commander and his lady before you leave."

"Thank you, Lieutenant."

"Pleasant dreams, sir." For some reason the young lieutenant gave Longarm a conspiratorial wink before he turned away.

Damn, Longarm hoped there were *some* secrets possible around here.

Otherwise it might be the post physician whose career was in deep shit after tonight.

He made his way around the dance floor to the colonel and his missus.

Chapter 14

To Longarm's amusement, the Visiting Bachelor Officers' Quarters was exactly as he'd left it, empty and untouched even though he'd been held up for three quarters of a damned hour by the nattering colonel and his incessant complaints about congressional appropriations.

The low-trimmed lamp still burned on the coffee table beside the sheaf of papers Lieutenant Colonel Harker's clerk had prepared. The bottle of Maryland distilled rye Longarm always traveled with sat on the table nearby.

There was no sign of Lenore Crane.

Longarm realized with mild surprise that he was disappointed. There was something about the girl that he'd liked.

Still, a young lady was entitled to a bit of teasing if she wished. He hoped he'd contributed a giggle or two to her evening.

The BOQ had no kitchen, but he found some glasses in a cabinet and poured a nightcap for himself. He almost hated to admit it about his favorite brand, but damned if the rye he'd had at the officers' mess wasn't even better. Maybe tomorrow he should find the mess sergeant over there and learn what label theirs was.

He dropped his Stetson onto the table and picked up the lamp and papers. He figured he could prop up in bed and read until he either finished the reports or got too sleepy to go on. Statements dictated by a career army officer weren't likely to be a light and snappy read.

Yawning, Longarm nudged the bedroom door open with a boot toe and went inside.

"Another six or seven hours and I might have gotten mad enough to leave," Lenore said.

"No disrespect intended, but, um . . ."

"I know. You thought I was a P.T." He decided he didn't even want to know how she'd come to learn the term "prick tease."

Lenore was sprawled in the middle of the narrow BOQ bed.

On top of the covers.

She hadn't a stitch on. Her ball gown and smallclothes were piled untidily on the only chair in the place. The underthings, he saw, were all plain and utilitarian garments. He was already beginning to believe that that wasn't at all appropriate for Miss Crane. She'd have been more at home with something that was lacy and slinky and designed to raise a man's blood pressure.

"Nice," he said admiringly as he brought the lamp closer and spent a moment inspecting what it was she had to offer. That stretched the truth a little, but fell short of being an actual lie.

Short and chunky when she was dressed, naked she was . . . short and chunky.

Her tits were plump little plums of flesh mounted on a thick torso. Her nipples were pink and pointy.

Her waist and thighs and ankles were disappointingly thick. But there was nothing at all wrong with the dark, curly bush at her vee. Nor with the flaps of pink flesh he could see hiding in there and peeking out through the hair.

She was ready, all right. The lamplight shined bright on a sheen of moisture to prove it.

He pointed and grinned. "What did you do, start without me?"

"I thought about it." She reached down and touched herself, spreading the lips of her pussy while he watched. She dipped a finger inside and then another, then she withdrew them, both gleaming wetly now, and rubbed her clitoris.

Her head arched back and tendons stood out on the side of her throat.

He saw the hard, shuddering pleasure ripple through her body as she brought herself to a climax. Lenore sighed and went limp on the bed.

"Shucks, you don't need me after all."

"It isn't the same," she said. "Besides, damn it, it's lonely."

"Reckon I can help out after all."

He set the lamp and papers down on the dresser and shucked his clothes.

"Oh, my," she said when Longarm stepped out of his balbriggans. "I *knew* there was some reason why I liked you."

"Should I take that as a compliment, ma'am?"

"Take it however you like. So long as you let me take this."

She reached out and touched him, drawing her hands gently up and down his shaft. "The last one I saw this nice was on a shire horse."

"Make you jealous, did it?"

"It would have except he was a gelding." She laughed and cupped Longarm's balls in one hand while she continued to fondle his shaft with the other.

"You're awful shy."

"But honest," she countered.

"I don't have any lambskins with me."

"That's all right. Daddy is a doctor, remember. I've already taken care of it. Now be quiet and let me enjoy myself."

"Yes, ma'am."

"That's better." She winked at him. Then leaned closer.

Longarm was standing beside the bed. Lenore scooted to the edge of it and sighed happily as she pressed his cock against her cheek. She turned her head and nuzzled him. He wasn't sure, but thought she seemed to be savoring the man-odor of him.

She lightly traced the length of him with the tip of her nose, then with the tip of her tongue. He wouldn't complain about the way either felt.

"Do you like?"

"I like," he assured her.

"Good, because I do too. There just isn't any substitute for the real thing. And believe me, I would know."

He decided to take Lenore's word for that and not ask for details.

She held his balls in both hands now. The sensation was warm. And not at all lonely. She licked the head of his cock like a kid licking a candy stick. Every time her tongue touched him his pecker responded with a little rise-and-fall jump. Lenore laughed and did it again.

Yeah, boredom did make them easy to amuse, Longarm thought.

"You're up to more than once in a night, aren't you?" she asked.

"If it's a contest you have in mind . . ."

She looked up at him with a wink, then dipped her head and took him into her mouth.

Longarm felt his knees sag and had to brace himself. Lenore Crane wasn't any kind of young innocent.

She drew him deep inside and applied a hard, insistent suction that he could feel all the way down into his balls.

"Not so quick," he cautioned. "This is too good to let it end right away."

She mumbled an answer that he couldn't begin to make out. But he thought she sounded pleased, which was all he'd intended anyhow.

Lenore's head bobbed up and down while she held her lips clamped firmly around him and continued that down-deep suction.

He reached down and fondled her head and the back of her neck, but was careful to not distract her from what she was doing. He wouldn't have wanted to do that.

"I'm gonna come if you don't back off mighty quick," he warned.

Instead of pulling away, Lenore quickened the pace. She squeezed his balls lightly and sucked even harder.

Longarm felt the rising swell of sensation deep in his groin.

It filled him until there was no longer any way to contain it, and then it spewed and spurted.

Lenore jammed her mouth onto him as far as she could manage and clung there. He could feel the pulsing movement of her throat as she swallowed. Her hands were still gentle on him, and still she stayed with him, sucking and making slurping noises until the last drop was spent.

"Whew!"

She nodded, then relaxed her pull on him and allowed him to slip wet and satisfied from her lips.

"Damn," she said.

"What's the matter?"

"I got so excited when I saw that pretty thing of yours that I forgot. I wanted to spend some time kissing you before I got started on the serious stuff, you being such a handsome gentleman."

"Oh, I bet we can work something out between us."

"What I'm hoping for is that we can work something *in* between us." She giggled and leaned forward again to lightly kiss the tip of his cock and then to lick away a final droplet of milky white fluid.

Lenore moved over to the other side of the bed, and Longarm lay down.

"Where are you going?"

She reached the far side of the bed and kept going, off the mattress and across the bedroom toward the sitting room. She winked at him but didn't answer.

When she came back she was carrying his bottle of rye.

She lifted the bottle to her mouth and took a healthy swig.

Longarm waited for her to hand the bottle to him, but apparently Lenore wasn't thinking of the liquor in terms of a beverage.

She swished the whiskey around and around in her mouth, making faces all the while, then turned and leaned down to spit it out into the slop jar beside the bed.

"Hey!" he yelped.

"But that stuff is *awful*. Really. I don't see how you men drink it."

"You mean—"

"No, don't even ask. Of course I don't drink. A proper young lady wouldn't *think* of doing so." Lenore laughed and flopped happily onto the bed at Longarm's side. Her tits bounced and her stomach quivered, and he could see that she was still plenty ready for a long and involved night to come.

But a decent young lady wouldn't ever think of taking a drink of liquor. No, sir. That wouldn't be acceptable at all.

Longarm chuckled and reached for her. He drew her to him and slipped his hand between her legs. She opened up just long enough to let him in, then clamped her thighs together, trapping him there. Not that he especially wanted to escape anyhow.

She kissed the side of his neck, then lifted her face to his. She tasted of rye whiskey, and that was all right.

"Mmmm-mm," Lenore breathed into his mouth.

"Yeah," he agreed.

Her pelvis began to rise and rotate as she pressed herself against him.

Longarm decided it was time he put his two cents worth in.

After all, it wouldn't be gentlemanly for him to lie there and make her do all the work.

And he did want to do the gentlemanly thing.

Chapter 15

Longarm woke early despite the late night he'd put in. After, that is, retiring early to bed. Not that he minded. The pillow beside him still smelled of Lenore's soap and powder and sweat.

He shaved and dressed quickly and carried Lieutenant Colonel Harker's reports with him to the officers' mess for breakfast.

With a full belly and that superb first cup of morning coffee he finally waded through the stilted, difficult language that told him in twenty pages the exact same information it had taken Harker half a minute to say yesterday. Ralph Frazier had been an outstanding cadet at the Academy at West Point, then had become an outstanding army officer, and finally had thrown it all away to follow a fruitless dream in a gray uniform.

The officer's old Point friend Harker had followed Frazier's career by way of rumor and word of mouth through Sibley's western campaign that had nearly captured the gold fields of what was then the Territory of Colorado.

Harker had heard no more of Major Frazier after the Colorado Volunteers sent General Sibley retreating back into Texas, and the lieutenant colonel, then still a captain in the Grand Army of the Republic, had assumed that his buddy died beside the many other Texans who'd failed to make it home from that almost-but-not-quite successful foray out of Texas.

The written report included a brief, blunt statement attesting that the man known lately as Raymond Frampton of Trinidad, Colorado, was in truth Ralph Anthony Frazier, graduate of the United States Military Academy, West Point, New York, a native of Victoria, Texas.

The remainder of the voluminous paperwork was a long, rambling reminiscence in praise of Frazier as a young and enterprising officer and gentleman.

Longarm forced himself to wade through every word of it.

According to Harker there never had been a hint of scandal attached to Cadet Frazier at the Academy. No after-hours drinking. No women friends smuggled into the dormitory. In fact, there was practically no color or character at all in Harker's report about Cadet Frazier, except for the fact that Frazier used to operate a small, free-enterprise commissary of sorts out of his luggage, stocking shaving soap and tooth powders and the like and selling them for a few pennies' profit to his fellow cadets.

There certainly was nothing in the report now that would give Longarm any clues as to how, and more important why, Ralph Frazier had ended up living in Trinidad under an assumed name. Or why the man might have abandoned his family there and wound up a murder victim sprawled in the dirt beside a lonely railway line in New Mexico Territory.

Longarm smoked a cheroot and had another cup of coffee while he bent his brain in search of some logical deductions on the subject.

Nothing came to mind. Nothing, at least, that made any sense on the surface of things.

But then the surface of this, he realized, was far from being all there was to it.

He finished his smoke, tucked the papers away, and said good-bye to the garrison officers who had been considerate enough to allow him the privacy of his thoughts, then made his way over to the telegraph room in the hope that some overnight responses might have come in.

Nothing had yet, either from Austin or from down the line where former Ranger Tom Jepp presumably had fled after murdering both Caswell and Frazier.

"I'll send a runner first thing if anything comes in for you, sir," the sergeant in charge of the message center promised. "The word is out that you're to be accommodated any way we can, sir."

"Thank you, Sergeant."

Longarm had more or less promised that he would stop by and see Harker this morning. And he certainly hadn't anything more pressing to do until the singing wires sang a song. He walked over to the post headquarters building and got directions to the adjutant's office.

It was still early in the day, but Lieutenant Colonel Harker had the look of a man who had already been bent over his desk for some hours. He stood with a smile and a handshake when Longarm came in. "Two coffees, Private. Do you take cream, Long? No? The coffees, Private, and, um, perhaps some crullers."

Longarm sure as hell couldn't complain about the cooperation he was finding at Fort Union.

"You've read my statements, Long?"

"Yes, sir."

"I hope they were helpful."

"They were, Colonel." The response was more polite than it was accurate.

"I presume you will want to interview that civilian employee Lieutenant Young told you about last night," Harker said.

"Yes, sir, I would." Longarm had no expectation that the talk would be helpful. But it couldn't hurt either. And interviewing a mulewhacker at least would be more interesting than sitting in the BOQ and twiddling his thumbs while he waited for word from Austin.

The coffee and crullers were delivered, and the post adjutant sent his orderly out on a second errand to find the civilian.

"The man's name is Moses Barnett. We employ him as a laborer in the warehouses, loading and unloading freight for transshipment to posts here in New Mexico and in western Texas and Arizona territory." It was no wonder Fort Union was so busy if they handled food and forage supplies for all the personnel over that wide an area. Supplies for disbursement to the reservation Indian tribes too if Longarm remembered correctly.

"Do you want to see Barnett's file, Deputy?"

"No, sir, I shouldn't think that would be necessary."

"It is available to you if you wish."

"Thank you, sir."

The orderly returned ten minutes or so later without Barnett. "Sorry, sir. This is Barnett's day off. I expect he'll be over at Loma Linda with his pals. Shall I send a detail for him, sir?"

Longarm could see that Harker was going to do just that, and there didn't seem any point in disrupting Barnett's day of rest. Even though it was likely the kind of rest day that a man would have to go back to work to get rested up from. "Don't bother, Colonel. I'll find him myself."

"As you prefer, sir," Harker said.

"Thanks for the coffee, Colonel."

"If there is anything else I can do, anything at all . . ."

"Yes, sir. You and your people have been most helpful, thanks."

Longarm walked back across the compound to the message center. The sun was hot on his shoulders now. The morning was advancing even if Custis Long was not.

"There you are, sir. I was just going to send a runner for you," the sergeant said when Longarm walked in.

Longarm's interest quickened. At last, dammit.

"Bad news, sir."

So much for getting hopes up. "What is it, Sergeant?"

"We have a break in our line somewhere, sir. Damn thing went out in the middle of a message for you from Denver. This is all we received before the line went dead, sir."

The sergeant handed over a slip of paper. The penciled message opened with the standard routing address, then read:

JURISDICTION APPROVED STOP PROCEED JEPP STOP AS ASIDE COMMA MISSUS VAIL DIAGNOSED

That was where it ended.

The sergeant responded to Longarm's scowls with profuse apologies. Which didn't do a damn thing to make Longarm feel any better.

What was Billy's wife diagnosed as having? Why couldn't

the sonuvabitch wire have held together for another lousy couple of words anyway?

Longarm grunted and groaned, but of course that wasn't going to help anything anymore than the sergeant's apologies did.

"I've sent a repair crew out already, sir," the sergeant said. "We should have the wire up again in a couple hours, three hours tops."

"Thank you, Sergeant," Longarm said as civilly as he could. Hell, it wasn't this man's fault.

He left the message center, stopped in the sunshine there for a moment, and decided he would rather have the activity of at least pretending to do something useful than sit around the post and stew in his own juices.

He turned and began walking toward the Gates of Hell.

What had Harker said that civilian's name was? It took Longarm a moment to recall it; he really hadn't been all that interested in talking to the man before. Barnett. Moses Barnett.

It couldn't hurt.

Chapter 16

Fort Union nowadays was brick and stone permanence.

Loma Linda looked like the entrepreneurs who'd built it expected to be kicked off their squatters' claims at any moment.

The place was a collection of trash heaped into piles and with canvas spread over the top for roofs. Close to being that bad anyhow.

There wasn't a structure in sight that could have cost its owner more than two dollars in materials and a few hours of light labor.

On the other hand, even in broad daylight Loma Linda was damn near as busy as the army post it so faithfully served.

Saloons, gambling dens, and fifty-cent whorehouses were open for business and busy doing that business.

Off-duty soldiers and teamsters yelped and shouted and reeled drunkenly through the bare dirt that passed as a main street.

The town wasn't prosperous enough—no, Longarm corrected himself, prosperity had nothing to do with it—the place wasn't permanent enough to bother erecting decent cribs for the cheaper class of two-bit whores. The women, mostly impoverished, pox-scarred Mexicans and Indians and Negresses, made do with roofless canvas privacy shields instead. They stood at the open front flaps of the make-do shelters and hawked their bodies with brazen directness.

Longarm glanced past a dark-skinned woman who had her tits on display and was trying to entice him with a raised skirt. The "floor" of her place was packed earth with a blanket folded in half and laid on the ground in lieu of a bed.

"A quarter, mistuh. Twenny-five cent for a quickie." The woman had pimples on her thighs, and there was an open sore drooling ooze beside her pussy.

Longarm figured he could resist her charms if he worked at it real hard.

Twenty-five cents for a piece of ass. Yet Loma Linda was thriving.

A private soldier earned, what, thirteen dollars a month and keep? A civilian laborer probably made a little more than that.

The thing was, there were an awful lot of those small paydays within walking distance of Loma Linda. And no place else for the men to spend their money. Probably a lion's share of the whole Fort Union payroll ended up here in the hands of the men who controlled the Gates of Hell.

He picked a saloon at random and walked into it. There were plenty of others he might have chosen, though.

"Yessir, what'll it be?"

"Beer." Longarm knew better than to order rye whiskey in a joint like this. The disappointment would have been doubly painful after the high-quality rye he'd been treated to last night in the officers' mess.

The barkeep handed over a tin mug of beer that was at least a third froth and charged a nickel for it. There was no free lunch laid out on the rough planks that served as a bar.

"Thanks," Longarm said, just like he meant it.

He carried his mug down the bar to a collection of men in civilian clothes. Did they know Moses Barnett? Hell, yes. Was he here today? One man thought so; the others hadn't seen Mose lately. He wasn't in this place anyway. Longarm thanked them and decided to go to the next joint. He gave his untasted beer to one of the civilians, deciding he didn't much feel like joining the revelry there today.

Three more saloons failed to turn up Moses Barnett.

"You won't find Mose here till he finishes emptying his balls, mister. Try the cribs," one man suggested. "Mose likes his pussy cheap an' regular."

Longarm thanked the man and turned back the way he'd just come.

It was approaching the noon hour, but no one in Loma Linda seemed interested in slowing down for dinner.

He saw a soldier with green corporal's chevrons on his sleeves saunter over to a cathouse—cathole would be more like it—line and peer drunkenly from one bawd to the next while he tried to make up his mind between them.

The two women smiled and simpered and showed him their pussies. They were doing fine until the corporal looked like he was going to take the woman on the right. Then the whore on the left got angry at being slighted and started cussing the winner in the contest for the soldier's two bits.

Cussing led to shouting and shouting led to shrieking, and two shakes later the two women were locked into a mutual bear hug and rolling on the ground. There was spit and loose hair flying as the women clawed and scratched and kicked at one another.

The corporal and half a dozen other men watched the fight for a while, then drifted away when the women got too tired to do much more than snarl at each other. The corporal, Longarm noticed, finally elected to go inside the shelter of an entirely different third whore to complete the Act of Love he'd come there for.

Life was good at Loma Linda, Longarm thought wryly.

He took up station between the string of whores and the saloons, and smoked a cheroot while he patiently buttonholed every civilian who stumbled by.

Eventually, he figured, one of them would turn out to be Moses Barnett.

Chapter 17

"You say you'll buy me a beer?"

"Uh, huh."

"Yeah, I got time to talk to you, I s'pose."

Longarm let Barnett lead the way to his favorite drinking establishment. Hell, as a regular maybe Barnett could even tell them apart. Longarm bought two beers and carried them to a corner where two small crates and one large one served as a table and chairs.

Moses Barnett was a man in his late fifties or thereabouts. Once he must have been a big, powerful man. He was still big but was going to seed now. His jowls sagged and his chest had fallen down so that it required a wide belt and big buckle to keep it from overflowing onto his trousers. He needed a shave and a haircut, and more than either of those needed a bath.

"Thanks, mister." Barnett tipped his mug back and drained it, then smacked his lips loudly and wiped his mouth on the back of his hand. Longarm pushed his mug across to Barnett, and the man grinned. "What was it you wanted to talk to me about?"

"I understand you used to ride with a Major Frazier in the Texas Mounted Volunteers," Longarm said.

"Ayuh, so I did. But I've had my voting right restored, you know. I took the oath 'long with most all the other boys. That was a long time back, mister. I hold no grudges."

"Neither does anyone else," Longarm assured him. "I'm a deputy United States marshal, Mr. Barnett. I'm investigating the murder of Major Frazier."

"The major got killed? I'm sorry to hear that, suh. Indeed I am. He was a pretty good ol' officer. Not that I knew 'im well, you understand. I was just an ol' boy with a carbine and an empty belly. We went wherever some officer pointed an' shot our guns when one of them hollered fire. I seen the major now and then, but I doubt I ever spoke a word with him. Still an' all, the boys thought of him as all right. I'm truly sorry to hear that he got himself killed." Barnett was working on his second beer hot and heavy.

Longarm hadn't expected much from this conversation. He decided it was just as well that he hadn't had any hopes to come crashing down now.

"When was the last time you saw Major Frazier, Mr. Barnett?"

"Oh, I dunno. You mind if I get another beer?"

Longarm gave Barnett a dime, and the laborer carried both mugs away for refills.

When he came back and sat down again Barnett said, "I believe the last I seen the major was in Apache Canyon. I don't believe I ever seen him again after that."

Longarm frowned. "Apache Canyon?"

"You wasn't with General Sibley nor Canby nor those crazy sons o' bitches from Colorado, I take it?"

"No, I wasn't in this part of the country then." Longarm was careful to avoid mention of just where he had been at the time.

"Mister, I don't know how the war was back East where there was regular troops. By the hundreds o' thousands, they tell me. Man, I can't imagine what fighting musta been like with so many people and guns and cannon. Out here was small potatoes in comparison. Or so everybody over at Union tells me, the ones that saw it. Me, all I know is what I seen myself, and that was enough to convince me that killing people ain't what I want to do for a living. You know?"

"I know," Longarm said.

"We mighta been small potatoes to the real army, but back then we thought we was something. We formed up in San Antonio. Two, three thousand of us, I'd guess. I was just a hick from the salt works at Indianola, and to me that army looked like all the men in Texas thrown into one bunch. I wanted to go with them, you understand. Nobody forced me to do it. My daddy and one uncle died defending Texas at Goliad, and I figured I could do the same wherever the general took us. Couldn't do any worse than them, anyhow, and in fact I done better. I came back from my war still alive." He shrugged and drank down half a beer.

"They put shiny new guns in our hands and a peck of cornmeal in our pokes and marched us up the Pecos Valley. They said we were headed to Colorado to liberate it from the damnyankees. No offense intended."

"None taken."

"We whipped Canby and his bluebellies at Santa Fe, and I got to say that that part of it was fun. Not the fighting part so much but what came later. I mean, we raised some hell in that town. Carried off everything that wasn't nailed down. Anything nailed down, we'd rip it loose and carry it off anyhow." Barnett winked. Longarm had the impression the man had already had more than just the few beers Longarm had bought for him.

"Women? Lordy, I reckon. Got so they'd see a Volunteer coming they wouldn't even wait to be grabbed. They'd lay down in the dirt and pull their skirts over their heads and just wait for it t' happen."

The fondness that came through Barnett's voice when he talked about that indicated that the most enlightening, or at least the most enjoyable, experience he'd gotten out of the war had been those rapes.

"I've always liked Mex'can pussy, mister, an' in Santa Fe even I got all I could handle. Free too. It was something, I'll tell you."

"I, uh, am sure it was."

"That only lasted so long, o' course. Pretty soon the general rounded us all up again, and we marched north. Never did make it to Colorado, though. Never got that far, damn it. They said there was gold in Colorado that we were gonna take. Women too, they said. But I wouldn't know about that. Never have been to Colorado.

"Territorial militia under some crazy son of a bitch named Chivington came down to meet us. They were just irregulars, mind, no better trained than we were. But Lordy, those boys could fight. I got to say, mister, that they took it to us.

80

"They met us down at Glorietta Pass. That isn't real far from here, but I've never been back and don't want to go neither. I didn't lose anything there that I'd want to find again. Just my dinner and about ten pounds of shit that I had to scrape out of my drawers after." He finished off the rest of that beer and reached for the other.

"I guess generals understand what happens in these things. I never did. I mean, one minute we're a column of Mounted Volunteers all full of piss and vinegar. Next thing you know there's guns banging and bugles ringing and we're a bunch of scared sons of bitches running every which way.

"And those bastard Coloradans everywhere you look. They must've had us outnumbered five, six, eight to one."

Longarm wasn't sure, but he thought he recalled hearing that it was the Colorado volunteers who'd been short on numbers. Not that that made any difference to the way Moses Barnett saw the battle from the back of his one horse.

"From there on it was one small bunch fighting with another small bunch and half the time getting in the way of some third small bunch. There were guns going off everywhere.

"They chased us back, mister. I got to say that they did. They broke us, and we turned tail and ran. There's those who would tell you to this day that we didn't do good, that we should have rallied and whipped them. Truth is, we did the best we could. I know I did, and I'd say the other boys did too. If there's shame in getting beat, then those Coloradans shamed us. I don't make excuses for it. We got beat."

He gulped down half the last beer and shook his head. "You were asking about Major Frazier, weren't you. I seen him now and then. A glimpse here. A look there. I mean, it wasn't like I was trying to guide on him or anything. Mostly what I was doing was trying to keep my ass from getting shot off and trying to shoot back whenever I seen a bluebelly to shoot at and wasn't too busy ducking.

"We were scattered all to hell, and I happened to be in the same bunch as the major. That's the only reason I saw him at all that day you see. We were trying to fight off the Coloradans and save our pack train. I guess they knew if they could get to our supplies and our loot they'd have us stopped. We couldn't go on to Colorado and take all that gold if we didn't have any food or powder to march and fight with, so they were deviling the pack train. Jumped us in Apache Canyon in a running fight back down toward Santa Fe, and I think that's the last time I ever did see the major. Not that I was looking for him in particular, you understand. But I don't recall seeing him again on the march back home. The bunch I was with was pretty small after that Apache Canyon fight. We didn't try and regroup. Never did see most of the rest of the fellows. We knew we were licked, so we cut away from the Santa Fe road and pointed ourselves back to the Pecos. We stopped at whatever ranches or rancherias we came across and provisioned that way. Bought food off the white men and took it off the Mex'cans."

Moses Barnett had been a real sweetheart in his day, Longarm thought, but didn't say.

"I never seen the major again after that, an' to tell you the truth never thought about him one way or the other. But I liked him good enough. I mean, he wasn't the kind of officer to get nasty with a fellow just for having a bit of fun. Like in Santa Fe some of the officers got mad at us for helping ourselves to a blowout, but Major Frazier never did. I guess he understood how things were for the ordinary guy and didn't begrudge a man having a little fun. If he even knew what was going on, that is. I wouldn't know about that." Barnett sighed and leaned back, tipping the last of the beer down his throat.

"All I know for sure, mister, is that I'm glad those days are a long while back and I don't have to worry anymore about crazy sons of bitches from Colorado coming at me with a gun." He winked. "O' course, I could do with some more of those Mex'can women spreading their legs open for free and with some o' those gold plates and candle holders and shit. But I'm not complaining. I come back from my war still breathing. My daddy didn't do that good. Are you, uh . . . ?"

"No, I'll be heading back to the post now," Longarm said, ignoring the not-quite-spoken request that Longarm pay for another round. "Thanks for your time." He didn't bother to add any thanks for the information, because that seemed even less valuable than Barnett's time had been.

With any kind of luck, Longarm thought, maybe the telegraph wire would be working again now and he could get on with things.

Chapter 18

The sergeant in charge of the message center was in a foul mood when Longarm returned.

"It's those damned Mexicans," he complained. "There's this bunch of crazy SOBs over at Mora. Some kind of religious cult, I think. They want all us Anglos to go home. They're harmless mostly, but every once in a while they go on a tear like this. My repair crew tells me somebody—has to be that crowd from Mora if you ask me—went up and down the railroad tracks tearing wire down every three or four poles. For miles, they did this. Now we got to clean up after them. If you ask me the colonel ought to send a detail over there and burn 'em all out. That would take care of it once and for all."

Sure it would, Longarm thought. And a fine policy it would be too. If you don't like your neighbor, burn the SOB's house down. Works every time. He lit a cheroot and contemplated with pleasure the fact that this particular problem was not his to worry about.

Better yet, maybe it would give the Fort Union commander something other than congressional appropriations to concern himself with.

"I've sent more crews out, Marshal," the sergeant said, finally coming around to the subject of interest. "It won't be long now that we know what we're dealing with."

"Thanks."

Longarm wandered outside, finished his smoke, and watched heavily laden freight wagons roll in and out of the post. It was a busy place. Longarm had to give them that much. Most folks seemed to think life on a quiet frontier consisted of soldiers sitting around drawing pay while they smoked their pipes. That might happen other places, but Fort Union was certainly busy enough.

Flour, cornmeal, bacon, salt pork, tinned beef, coffee, sugar, and livestock fodder moved in quantities that were . . . enough to feed an army. There was considerably less emphasis, Longarm noticed, on cartridges and cannon shells. The southern tribes were quiet indeed.

Across the parade ground Longarm could see a trio of young ladies taking a stroll—they were too far away for him to tell if Lenore was among them—and closer by, a guardhouse detail lazily poked the hard ground with sticks, pretending to police up litter while they enjoyed the sunshine.

The garrison flag hung limp on its staff, stirring only now and then as a puff of breeze lifted it.

"Marshal?"

Longarm tossed his cigar butt down—give the prisoner squad something to pounce on—and turned.

"Sar'nt said to tell you we have a link t' the south now, sir. There's a urgent message for you."

"Thanks." Longarm stretched his legs getting back inside the telegraph center.

Las Vegas was a settled community, older than the railroad that now served it, and older too than the army post seventeen miles to the north. It had gracious homes and tree-lined streets and some of the finest saddle makers to be found anywhere. Longarm had been there before and liked it.

The army ambulance supplied by Lieutenant Colonel Harker was drawn by a fast team that made the distance at a run. The driver deposited Longarm at City Hall.

"The lieutenant said I was to wait for you if you need, sir."

"Don't bother to do that," Longarm said as he swung down to the ground.

The driver's face fell.

"Tell you what, son. Why don't you wait around town in

85

case I happen to change my mind and need that ride back to Union. Hang around, say, three or four hours before you start back."

The driver grinned and gave him a wink.

"Thank you, sir."

By then Longarm was paying no attention to the soldier. He was hurrying into City Hall in search of the Las Vegas police chief.

A stocky, heavily muscled man of middle age looked Longarm over and said, "You're Long?"

"That's right."

The chief extended a hand to shake. "I'm Carl Worley. Pleased to meet you. Call you Longarm, don't they?"

"Most do."

"I'm Carl. Or Hey you. Not Chief, please. Makes me feel like a wild Injun every time somebody calls me that, and I had all I wanted of Injuns when I was a young man. Too old for that nonsense now."

"Fair enough," Longarm agreed.

While the amenities were being dispensed with, Chief Worley was leading Longarm out of the tiny police station and down a hall to a doorway that looked like it led to a closet.

"Down here, Longarm."

The closet turned out to be a set of steep and narrow stairs leading into a basement. The underground chamber was chilly and smelled of moist dirt.

"I told the undertaker to keep his hands off till you had time to take a look. This is the coolest place we could think of to put him until we found you."

There was one lantern burning in the dank basement. Chief Worley lit two more and hung them from nails so Longarm could get a better look at the corpse that was laid out on some planks.

"Figured I'd best call you in once I saw who the dead man was, Longarm."

"I appreciate it, Carl."

Longarm tipped his hat back and took a moment to look things over.

The undertaker had been chased away, but he or someone

else had already had time to undress the body and begin cleaning it before the police chief's orders were issued.

A naked corpse is always an ugly thing, Longarm reflected. Ugly pale and ugly shriveled.

A dead cock is no more than a small scrap of useless flesh, impossible to think of as having once been hard and proud and lusty.

The dead man had been slender and of average height. He was clean-shaven and had thinning gray hair. The eyes were closed, held shut by large copper pennies now, so Longarm could not see what color they had been.

The hands were large for the man's frame, with long, slender fingers. The nails had been bitten to the quick and now looked inflamed and painful even though there would be no more pain for this man.

The toes were unusually long too, with lumpy nails too long uncut. Hair sprouted from the toe knuckles.

A man has neither privacy nor dignity in death.

"You're sure of the identification, Carl?"

"No question about it, Longarm. I knew him myself. Hell, most lawmen on this side of New Mexico knew him. It shocked me when I heard he'd switched sides, let me tell you."

"Shocked a lot of people," Longarm agreed.

He moved closer to the corpse and looked again.

It didn't take much expertise to see how the man had died.

There was a blue and purple indentation, washed clean of blood and brains now, square in the center of the forehead, and a considerably larger exit wound on the back left quarter of the skull. The slug had penetrated at an angle, then smashed its way out again. A large-caliber weapon then. A bullet from one of the small rimfires wouldn't have had enough force to pass clean through the heavy bone of the skull.

"Rifle possibly," Worley said. "A deliberate execution, whatever gun was used." Longarm too could see the powder burns surrounding the entry wound. "Rope marks on the wrists there too. Hard to see now in this light and after the washing, but they were clear when I first saw him. Look closer."

Longarm did. He could see the faint indentations and now-pale abrasions.

"Son of a bitch tied his hands and then killed him."

"Uh, huh," Worley agreed. "Like I said. I call it an execution."

"You've seen a murder victim before, I'd take it."

"Now and then," the police chief agreed. "But not so many mysteries about them around here. What we usually get is two fellas drunk and pissed off shooting at each other for no good reason, or sometimes a man taking an ax to his old woman or the old woman taking her potato peeler to the cheating husband. That sort of thing. Not generally anything like this."

Longarm nodded and moved around the makeshift bier so he could look the corpse over from new angles. He didn't see anything that Worley hadn't already spotted.

"Where'd you find him, Carl?"

"In his hotel room. He was dressed at the time, of course. I have the clothes and personal effects in my office upstairs. His luggage is still in the hotel. I left everything undisturbed there except for taking out the body and whatever he had on him at the time. I put an officer on the door to keep people out until I could get you here."

Longarm nodded. "You're efficient. Thanks."

"All rubes aren't stupid, you know."

"Thank goodness." Longarm smiled and added, "Rube."

Worley chuckled, taking no offense. "City boy," he said.

Longarm laughed.

He stepped closer to the corpse and lifted the right hand, examining the fingernails more closely. They had been bitten down so far it was impossible to tell now if the dead man had been able to put up a fight before he was tied. There were no visible abrasions on the knuckles, and the nails were not long enough to have caused a scratch on the killer.

Something else occurred to Longarm, and he levered the dead man's jaw open. The tongue was a pale shade of purple. There were a few teeth missing, but those losses were not recent.

"Hold a light closer would you please, Carl?"

Worley took down one of the lanterns and held it close to the open mouth.

"Little higher, please?" Longarm grunted and reached in past the teeth. The mouth was cool and felt oddly dry. The sensation was fairly unnerving.

"Did you find something?"

"I think so. Bring the light closer?" Worley moved the lantern close enough that Longarm could feel the heat radiating from its globe. "There."

He plucked out a quarter-inch-long scrap of thread and lint and held it up for Worley to see.

"I missed that, damn it. He was gagged."

"Uh, huh. Tied, gagged, and neatly done away with. I don't suppose anyone heard anything."

"Not a sound. I talked to the salesman who was in the room next door. The fellow says he went to bed fairly early and never heard any gunshots. He did hear some thumping in the room sometime during the night, but the sounds didn't last long. He's sure there was no gunshot. He left his room and went down to breakfast about six this morning, and all the other guests on that floor were downstairs by seven or thereabouts. The way I see it, the killer must have waited until the back part of the hotel was emptied this morning and then fired just the one shot. You know how that is. Two shots people hear. One shot only makes them wonder if they've heard something. They look up, and if they don't hear a second noise figure it wasn't anything after all and forget about it."

Chief Worley definitely wasn't any backwoods rube, Longarm realized. He understood human nature—and police work—right well.

"You know the thing I can't understand, Carl?" Longarm frowned. "What the fuck was a wanted murderer like Tom Jepp doing in a Las Vegas hotel room when he should've been hightailing it the hell away from here?"

"Puzzling, ain't it," Worley agreed placidly.

But then the full impact of this case wasn't his to worry over.

"Let's go upstairs," Longarm said.

The police chief blew out all the lights except for the one

low-trimmed lantern that had been burning when they came down into the basement. Then he and Longarm climbed back up to the better light and the cleaner air of the City Hall offices above.

Former Texas Ranger Tom Jepp's corpse lay cold and silent in the cellar below.

Chapter 19

"I can't get a handle on this case," Longarm admitted as he opened the box of clothing and personal effects Chief Worley had set in front of him.

"I *thought* I had it figured." He outlined for Worley the sequence of events that had started in Trinidad and now were taking strange new directions in Las Vegas. "I figured Tom Jepp for my murderer and both Caswell and Frampton, who turns out to be Frazier, as having some previous connection with Jepp.

"But if any of that was so, what the hell was Jepp doing in a hotel room here and why was he murdered? And by who?"

"If you're telling me all this because you're expecting some bright theories out of me, Longarm, then I have to disappoint you." Worley smiled. "On the other hand, if all you want is sympathy I'll be glad to oblige. The case is one weird sonuvabitch and no doubt about it."

"Thank you ever so much," Longarm groaned.

He pulled bloodstained clothing out of the box and examined each piece before setting it aside. All the pockets were empty, and there was nothing hidden inside the seams or linings that Chief Worley hadn't already found.

A wooden cigar box inside the larger container held everything the chief had taken out of Jepp's pockets or off his person.

Longarm grunted with satisfaction but no surprise when he saw a long, slim-bladed pocketknife in the cigar box. He picked it up and examined it, then pulled the blade open.

The knife was a good five inches long when closed and nearly double that when opened. The single blade, which had a spring-loaded mechanism to lock it in position when open, was little more than a quarter-inch wide but unusually thick. About halfway, Longarm thought, between an ice pick and a stiletto.

"Funny-looking thing," he said, holding it up to the light. There were dark red stains near the base of the blade. The coloring might have been rust. Longarm was sure it was blood. The blood of K. C. Caswell and Ralph Frazier, in fact.

"I saw one something like it once," Worley said, "although that one wasn't a folding knife. Had a blade like that, though. Belonged to a trapper I knew."

Longarm frowned. "Damned odd skinning knife."

"It wasn't for skinning. He used it to kill his catch with. One poke into the back of the neck just under the skull and it would kill quick and clean and not ruin any fur. Handy too for chopping holes in ice on a stream so you could make a beaver set."

"I wonder if Jepp used to do some trapping."

"Never heard him say anything about it if he did, but Tom was the kind of fellow would tackle anything if he once took an interest in it. Especially anything outdoors. I wouldn't be surprised if he did some trapping."

"Probably never know now, but I'd say this has to be the weapon that he used on Caswell and Frazier. It fits what I saw of their wounds."

"Which means your case is closed, Longarm, and Jepp's murder belongs to me. Jepp killed your man with the federal want on him. Now Jepp is dead too. You can call this one closed and go home if you like."

Longarm looked at the Las Vegas police chief, but he saw no disapproval in the man's expression. Worley was only trying to be helpful. Offering him an easy way out if that was what Longarm wanted.

"Tom Jepp was a fugitive with federal wants on him too now, Carl. I call his murder interference with the duties of a federal officer. If you want me out of it, you'll have to get a court order to deny my jurisdiction. And if you want to do that, Carl, I expect I'll appeal the court order."

Worley grinned. "You won't find me sitting on a court bench when I don't have to. I just wanted to know how things stood."

"All right then."

It took a moment for Longarm to figure out the locking mechanism and close the knife. He dropped it onto the table and went through the other things that Jepp had had on him when he died.

There were coins totaling $26.14 and a draft on an Austin, Texas, bank for another $173.

"Closed out his bank account when he took off, I'd say," Worley observed. "It seems damn little for a peace officer's life savings, don't it?"

"Yeah."

There were a gilt brass stickpin and a cheap pocket watch. A bandanna. Pipe, tobacco pouch, and matches.

Very little indeed to show for a lawman's life's work.

But then, Longarm realized, there wouldn't be that much difference if it was Worley and Jepp going through a dead Custis Long's things.

And until recently, Jepp had had a good reputation as a lawman.

What the *hell* had changed that?

Longarm opened the tobacco pouch and rooted through it, but the leather pouch held nothing but loose tobacco.

"There's no badge," Longarm noted, "and no gun."

"He wasn't a Ranger anymore," Worley reminded him.

"Yeah, but he still had his badge with him. He showed it to Amos Kronnenburg up in Trinidad when he claimed Caswell for extradition."

"The badge must be over in the hotel room with his luggage and the gun. We'll go over and take a look whenever you're ready."

Longarm piled everything back into the box. "Let's go."

"He checked in alone," the night desk clerk said. He had been off duty when Worley was at the hotel earlier, so the man hadn't yet been interviewed. "You can see for yourself where he signed the register." He opened the book, turned to the next to last page of it, and spun it to face the two lawmen.

"Tom Jones?" Longarm asked.

The clerk shrugged but made no apologies. Here a man was entitled to be whoever and whatever he said he was.

"You didn't know him?" Worley asked.

"No, Chief, I never saw the man before last night. He came in about nine, asked for a room, and paid in advance for two nights."

"Two nights?"

"Yes, sir. He said he might need the room longer."

"Was he carrying his own luggage or was he with a porter?" Longarm asked.

"He was alone. There hadn't been a train come in for several hours. Most men who come in on a train come get their rooms first thing, then go do whatever else they need. We generally know the train passengers because of how quick they get here from the station. We can almost count on customers twenty minutes after we hear the whistle."

Jepp had intended to stay at least two nights in Las Vegas. And he'd already been in town for some time before he took the hotel room. He would have been in Las Vegas the better part of a full day already, Longarm realized, because of the timing between when Ralph Frazier was murdered and when that train would have reached Las Vegas.

What the hell was so important here that Jepp failed to continue his flight from two murders so he could make an extended layover in Las Vegas?

"Did he have any visitors? Did you see him with anyone else or talking to anyone else?"

"I can't say if he did or he didn't, only that I didn't notice him with anybody else and that nobody asked for him at the desk here."

"Did he go outside again after he checked in?"

"Not that I saw. But then there's at least two ways out of the hotel that I can't see from the desk. He could've gone out, but I don't know that he did or didn't. If he went out, he kept his key with him."

Longarm grunted. He looked at Chief Worley, but got back only a shrug. The two turned toward the stairs.

"If it helps anything," the clerk volunteered, "Mr. Jones acted kind of excited. Tired, I'd say, but excited too. Like a man holding a straight flush when everybody else at the table is wanting to pay big to see his hand."

"Thanks," Longarm said.

"We may want to talk to you some more," Worley added. "Don't go anywhere that I can't find you."

"Yes, sir."

The young police officer posted outside the hotel room door had managed to find himself a chair to sit on and a book to read, and he was drawing pay for sitting there and reading. He looked almost disappointed when his boss and Longarm showed up.

"You can go home now, Ron. This is Deputy Marshal Long. We'll take it from here."

"Yes, sir." The officer closed his book and picked up the chair to return it to wherever it belonged.

The hotel room was unlocked. It was also fairly gory.

There wasn't any question where Tom Jepp had been when he died. Blood and dried brain matter covered the floor and wall under a window. The bed nearby was unmade and had been slept in by someone who had been restless.

Jepp's gunbelt lay on top of the dressing table. The loaded Colt was in its holster, and the belt was neatly wrapped around the holster and gun. Jepp's Ranger badge was pinned to the leather strap that held the holster together. The badge hadn't been visible until the belt was unwrapped from the holster. A battered suitcase sat on the floor beside the dresser.

There was no rifle, Longarm noticed, and no saddle. He wondered if Jepp had stored those somewhere or sold them. Possibly he would never know either way.

"Messy," he said.

"The murderer could have pressed the muzzle against Jepp's forehead. That would have partly muffled the sound. He didn't use a pillow, though, unless he brought his own. I already looked."

"Okay, thanks."

Longarm picked up the suitcase, carried it to the foot of the bed, and opened it.

The contents of the bag were no more informative than the contents of Jepp's pockets had been. Less perhaps because at least the box of body effects had turned up the knife Jepp had used in the murders he'd committed before he became a murder victim himself.

The suitcase held only articles of clothing, a comb, toothbrush, a box of tooth powder, and a box of .45 cartridges.

"Not very damn helpful," Longarm said.

"No," Worley agreed. He turned to the dresser and started going through the drawers.

While the police chief was doing that, Longarm knelt beside the mess on the floor and began digging at the baseboard with the tip of his knife blade.

"Did you find something?"

"Just wanted to get a look at the slug."

Longarm dug it out of the wood, frowned, and tossed it to Worley.

"That isn't going to tell us much."

"No, dammit." The slug now was a misshapen lump of lead that might once have been any size or shape. Its passage twice through bone and once into wood had left nothing that was recognizable as to caliber or type.

"Anything in the drawers?"

"Nothing but lint. He never unpacked a thing."

"Even though he figured to be here for two days," Longarm observed.

"He had to know he was wanted for murder already. Maybe he wanted to be ready to grab and run."

Longarm looked out the hotel room window. There was a porch roof directly under the window. A man could slip out the window, across the shallow pitched roof, and down into the alley below if he wanted to get away from someone in the hall.

On the other hand, Longarm reflected, that route could work in two directions. A man who wanted into the hotel room without being seen would have been able to get in that way.

The window was unlocked, and moved freely up and down when Longarm tried it.

Was Tom Jepp here for the purpose of finding and murdering yet another man and had the tables been turned on him by surprise?

Or was there some other explanation for Jepp's death?

Longarm wished he knew the answer to that one.

He sighed. Shit, he wished he knew the answer to *any* of the questions he had about this string of deaths.

"Let's go, Carl. I think I need some supper and a strong drink or three."

"You buy three, I buy three, and between us, Longarm, we'll be able to solve all the world's problems before we're done." Worley picked up the suitcase that had belonged to Tom Jepp and led the way back down the stairs.

Chapter 20

"Why, dammit?" Longarm complained. "Why didn't he run when he had the chance? Why'd he stop here and get himself killed?"

Carl Worley didn't bother to answer. But then he hadn't bothered to answer it the last ten or twenty times Longarm had asked it either. Worley shrugged, picked up his glass, and said, "Have another."

"Don't mind if I do."

It was Worley's turn to buy. The police chief got up from the table and walked with exaggerated care to the bar for the refills.

The rye whiskey they served here hadn't tasted all that good to begin with. But it was commencing to go down smoother as the evening wore on.

Longarm frowned and shook his head and asked himself the same question again. He didn't answer himself, though. He couldn't. He sighed and reached for the glass Worley put down in front of him. "Thanks." He tipped the glass back and drank off half of it. The whiskey was even more warming than the bowl of green chili they'd had for supper had been. And the chili had been about half jalapeño peppers, or so Longarm had thought at the time.

"To your good health," Worley said as he knocked his drink back.

"Yeah," Longarm growled. "So why'd he do that, Carl?"

"Why'd who do what?"

"Never mind."

Longarm looked up and blinked. There was somebody standing beside the table. Longarm was sure he'd never seen the man before. The fellow was thin and pale and looked unhealthy. His clothes were ragged and dirty, and he needed a shave. The red veins in his nose and the rheumy ooze weeping out of his eyes said he was the town drunk. Longarm sympathized with him. The whiskey here had a helluva kick to it.

"Thought this here thing might interest you, Chief," the man was saying. "Thought you might wan' it fer your collection. I'd sell it t' you, Chief. Cheap, seein' as it's you."

He held a rusty lump of a thing under the police chief's eyes. The drunk's expression was hopeful. "Fifty cents, Chief? It's gotta be worth fifty cents t' you. Be real nice in yer collection, eh?"

Worley sniffed and shook his head. "You know I don't want any trash like that, Ed."

"A quarter, Chief? It's gotta be worth a quarter. Worth more'n that for trade bait, huh?"

"Look, Ed, you go tell Henny I said you can have a drink on my tab. But I don't want that stupid thing. Go on now. I'm busy here."

"Thank you, Chief, thank you." The drunk bobbed his head obsequiously and backed away, turning and hurrying to the bar for the promised drink.

Longarm frowned. It was a rusty, busted little pepperbox revolving pistol that the drunk had been trying to palm off. Probably something he'd scrounged out of a trash dump somewhere.

So why was a thing like that all of a sudden grabbing Longarm's interest?

Longarm was feeling too drunk himself right now to call it to mind. But there was *some*thing. . . .

"Carl!" he blurted out.

"Um?"

"Did you show me everything you recovered off of Tom Jepp's body?"

"Off the body and in the room, Longarm. You seen what there was to see."

"Everything?"

"Yeah, sure. There wasn't all that much to see."

"There wasn't an old, antique pistol in his things, was there?"

"Only the Colt in his holster. I didn't take a thing out of that room 'cept what you seen in my office before."

The whiskey fog in Longarm's brain cleared away like morning river mist when a hard breeze springs up.

"Damn!"

"What's the matter?"

"No offense, Carl, but could one of your officers have taken home a souvenir from that hotel room? Or maybe whoever found the body could've lifted something before he reported it?"

Worley shook his head. "No chance. Not to either of them ideas, Longarm. The body was found by the cleaning lady, and all she done when she opened that door was stand an' scream. I'd be willing to swear she never foot inside the room. If she had, it would have been Jepp's money she was interested in, not some antique pistol. As for my officers"— he shook his head again—"I was there on the scene not twenty paces behind my first officer. I'm sure I'd know it if anybody got light-fingered in there."

"But, dammit, there oughta be an old Paterson Colt in Jepp's things."

"Paterson? Now I damn sure know I'd've spotted one of those if there'd been one lying around. Not so many of them around, you know. I have a .31-caliber in my gun collection, and I'd damn sure be interested in finding other models to hang alongside that one."

"Up in Trinidad, Carl, Caswell stole a presentation-grade Paterson from an old man he murdered. That's what he was in jail for when Jepp went up and sprung him with Frazier's help. And when he got Caswell off the town marshal there, he demanded to take the Paterson with him as evidence. The gun was turned over to him along with Caswell. Now all three of those fellows are dead and their bodies strung across one state and another territory. But there's no sign of that old Paterson in with Jepp's personal effects, and it wasn't found with either of the other bodies either."

"I can't tell you where it is, Longarm, but I can sure tell you where it isn't. And that's in my office or in that hotel room where Tom Jepp was killed. I haven't seen any Paterson Colt except my own in five, six years or longer."

"Shit," Longarm said. "If something was gonna be stolen off those dead men, why would it be a junky old gun that won't even fire? None of them was robbed. There was cash found on Jepp and Frazier both. Enough to make a robbery worth the while. Yet the money wasn't taken."

"You said this Paterson was a presentation-grade—"

"But in lousy condition," Longarm added. "It was pretty beat-up. At least that's what I'm told."

"A presentation-grade Paterson in good condition might fetch twelve dollars. Fifteen absolute tops. An ordinary Paterson in decent firing condition would be worth a buck and a half, two dollars. A junker?" Worley shrugged. "Two bits if there are some parts that could be useful to repair another old gun. The one I've got at home I bought for six bits, and it's in pretty nice shape."

"There's two things you could do that might help me, Carl," Longarm said.

"Name them."

"One, put the word out to your people that they should look for a beat-up old Paterson Colt and put the arm on anybody they see with one. The other thing, I think you should start looking around and see if any citizens from here turn up missing."

Worley raised an eyebrow.

"Tom Jepp abandoned a solid Ranger career to go off and do whatever it was he was doing here. Same deal with Frazier. He walked away from a family and a judicial bench to come south with Jepp. This *has* to be something important, Carl. I'm thinking that if Jepp was murdered here it's because his killer is a part of whatever brought those others down already. And if it's big enough to be worth them throwing their lives away for it, it'd be big enough for this Las Vegas man to do the same. Look for somebody . . . I don't know, it doesn't have to be anybody prominent or important; after all, Caswell was an ex-con just released from Canon City . . . look for somebody who's gone missing for no reason at all. Missing-person complaints, houses left sitting empty, business locked up . . . could be anything at all. But I'm thinking maybe that's what we have to look for now. A local man gone missing. And when we find him we'll see does he have a Paterson Colt in his back pocket."

Worley too seemed sober and alert now that there was serious business to be done. "I'll get my people on that right away, Longarm. What d'you figure to be doing in the meantime?"

"I'm gonna go back to Fort Union, Carl, and have another talk with that fella Barnett. Couple more things I want to ask him."

"Anything I can do to help?" Worley asked.

"The use of a horse and saddle would be good."

"Let's go see to it." Worley was on his feet and heading for the door immediately. The Las Vegas police chief wasn't a man to let the grass grow when it was time to quit playing and do some work. "I have a horse and saddle you can borrow. Then I'll rattle my boys around and get them to asking questions. If there's anybody in town who's not where he ought to be, Longarm, I'll know about it before daybreak."

Longarm was beginning to think there weren't a lot of men he would pick to work with over and above Carl Worley. The man was the sort who wanted to get things done and do them right.

Longarm followed him to a small stable set behind a lovely home on a tree-lined street. Worley gave him a saddle and the better of the two horses the chief kept, then waved good-bye and started off in the direction of City Hall and the police headquarters there while Longarm bumped the chief's leggy bay into a long trot for Fort Union.

Chapter 21

It was ten o'clock or so by the time Longarm reached Fort Union. Not late but not working hours either. The warehouse area where Moses Barnett worked was silent except for the slow, bored footsteps of a guard detail. The corporal of the guard had no idea where Barnett lived and suggested Longarm try first at Loma Linda. Longarm put the horse into motion again.

Loma Linda at night was even busier than Loma Linda during the day. Depending on how lucky they felt at the moment, the off-duty soldiers, teamsters, and civilian employees from the army post were either gulping beer, bucking the faro dealer, or lined up waiting a turn at one of the whores.

It was kinda funny, Longarm thought, how sour-faced and serious these fellows looked when it was fun they'd come here to find. Obviously, though, there'd been a payday recently and these boys were bent on getting rid of their income just as fast as they could manage it.

For the convenience of those who weren't good spenders, the good folks who ran Loma Linda provided two-legged alley rats capable of emptying a pocket all at once courtesy of a weighted sap and a tap on the noggin.

Longarm rode into the middle of a fuss with one of those when he entered the Gates of Hell.

Carl Worley's bay horse shied and reared as a dust devil came swirling out of an alley mouth.

Longarm brought the horse back down onto its feet and took a look. The dust devil turned out to be a cloud raised by a dozen men or more, all of them busy pummeling one sad-looking little weasel who was the center of their attentions.

"Hold on, dammit," Longarm barked.

The soldiers responded to the command in Longarm's tone of voice and quit beating their hapless victim. They stood looking up at him expectantly. "Sir?"

"What's this all about, Sergeant?"

The quartermaster sergeant hooked a thumb toward a private who had blood running down his neck and fury in his eyes. "This civilian thumped Jamison on the head with a billy, sir, an' tried to rob him. What the sonuvabitch didn't know, sir, is that Private Jamison wasn't all that drunk yet, an' besides has the hardest head in this man's army. The private grabbed hold o' him, sir, an' hollered for the rest of us to come help. We was, uh, providing the civilian with corrective discipline when you come upon us. Sir."

Discipline was one likely word for it. Longarm took a closer look at the civilian, who was dangling from the fist of a particularly large and ugly infantry corporal with sky-blue stripes and piping on his sleeves.

The would-be alley thief had a face that looked like raw meat now and would for some little time to come. The man's nose had been given a new section of face to ride on, and his bloody, swollen hands looked like most if not all his fingers had been busted. One ear was torn mostly away from the side of his head and was flapping loose against his cheek. If he came away with any sight remaining in his left eye he was going to be lucky.

"Is there any civilian law here, Sergeant?" Longarm asked.

"No, sir."

That did complicate matters. The officers at Fort Union wouldn't want to assume authority over any civilians except their own employees, and this battered little pickpocket wasn't likely to be on anybody's payroll.

Longarm quite frankly didn't want to start enforcing the peace in Loma Linda either. That would be a full-time and thankless job, and there wasn't any federal jurisdiction he could claim—make that none that he was required to claim—even if he had been inclined in that direction.

"Form a detail, Sergeant," Longarm snapped.

"Sir?" The quartermaster sergeant did draw himself to rigid attention, though. Either he already knew who the deputy was or the man was taking no chances that Longarm might be an out-of-uniform officer.

"Take four men and escort the civilian out of the area. Impress upon him the wisdom and the health benefits of long walks, Sergeant. One-way walks, that is."

The sergeant began to smile.

"No more beating, though, and no more broken bones," Longarm cautioned. "But if your escort detail happens to stumble and fall now and then, I will understand that the night is dark and the path difficult, um?"

"Yes, *sir!*" The sergeant snapped a salute that Longarm had no right to return but did anyway.

The quartermaster sergeant executed a smart about-face—the wonder was that he would remember how after years in supply—and stabbed a finger at the four biggest, beefiest soldiers in the mob. "Form detail," he bawled. "Take, uh, civilian." There wasn't any actual command appropriate to the occasion, but the improvisation worked well enough. The four soldiers each grabbed hold of a protruding limb on the pickpocket and lifted. "At the quick march, forward . . . ho."

The garbage detail squared their shoulders, hiked their chins, and marched off down the road and out of town with the quartermaster sergeant marching beside and calling cadence for them.

Longarm hoped the thief survived the experience. More or less.

"Carry on, gentlemen," Longarm said to the remaining soldiers. He touched the brim of his Stetson and moved on to the center of the wild and woolly little squatter town.

Longarm wasn't willing to claim with any certainty that Moses Barnett was not in Loma Linda tonight.

But he was willing to concede that he couldn't find the man tonight.

He talked to several people who knew Barnett, but their opinions were divided on the subject of whether or not the man was sharing the fun on this particular evening. No one had seen him recently in any event.

Longarm eventually was forced to conclude that it would be easier and more efficient to wait until morning and find Barnett at work than to waste any more time looking for him in Loma Linda.

He swung back onto Worley's horse and pointed the animal's nose back in the direction of the fort. He hoped that BOQ room was still available, because it had been a long and frustrating day. What he wanted now was a drink and about ten uninterrupted hours of sleep.

Chapter 22

Longarm grinned. The BOQ was undisturbed since he'd left it. With one exception.

Lenore Crane was stretched out under the covers in his bed and was sleeping soundly. He could see her hair spread out across the pale shadows of the pillow even in the darkness of the bedroom.

She must have figured he was coming back tonight even if Longarm hadn't particularly planned on it.

Longarm wasn't all that unhappy now to discover that she'd been right.

He chuckled and undressed silently in the darkness, then padded quietly on bare feet to the side of the bed. He placed his Colt on the nightstand and slipped underneath the sheet at Lenore's side.

He had no way to judge how long she'd been sleeping, but he could damn well tell that her sleep was a deep one now.

Her breath fluttered softly with a sound that was just short of being a snore. When the bed tilted with his weight Lenore stirred but did not waken.

He wriggled stealthily closer until he could feel the warmth of her skin.

There were options here. He was tempted to put his lips next to her ear and let out a war whoop.

That would get the job done, all right. On the other hand, causing a heart attack wasn't much what he had in mind.

And besides, some women tended to wake up grumpy when a fella got playful.

He propped his head on one hand and lay there contemplating the possibilities.

Lenore was naked. He could feel the smooth skin of her back pressing soft against his belly.

Would she like . . . ? Or then again might he . . . ?

The problem was solved for him.

The thoughts he was thinking led inevitably to an erection as he anticipated the pleasures Lenore was able to give and to demand.

The hard, warm shaft extended outward from his crotch and bridged the short gap that separated them.

Almost as if the thing had a will of its own it found a nesting place beneath the crack of Lenore's round ass.

The rhythm of Lenore's breathing changed when the head of Longarm's cock burrowed between her legs from behind.

She sighed and pressed her face into the pillow. Longarm wasn't sure, but he thought she was smiling.

He nudged forward just a little. There was dry resistance at first. Then the moisture from Lenore's ever-ready box slicked things up a bit and he could slide forward easier again.

He chuckled and lay still as again she stirred, and he thought she was going to wake up. After a moment her breathing steadied and she returned to a state of deep sleep.

Longarm pressed forward at the hips another fraction of an inch.

The head of his cock lay against the lips of her pussy like a sausage in a bun. He could feel the tantalizing wet heat of her, and the head of his pecker bumped and throbbed lightly in time to his heartbeat.

Lenore snuffled and snorted and shifted position, curling her knees up and burying the side of her head into the pillow.

Longarm smiled and scooted an inch or so lower on the mattress to gain a better angle. The head of his cock was still pressed warm and comforting against Lenore's pussy.

He pulled back. Just a bit. And then forward. Just a bit.

He felt the head slide in between the wet lips. He stiffened and held himself still, thinking that small penetration might waken her, but it didn't.

Smiling again he gently pushed, and another eager inch found comfort.

Then another.

He paused, enjoying the sensations of moist heat that were surrounding him now. Then he moved his hips forward and socketed himself the rest of the way inside her.

Lenore came awake with a start and made a soft, mewling sound deep in her throat.

She giggled and pushed her ass backward, tight against his belly, claiming all of him within her now.

Her hand crept behind her, fumbled its way underneath the sheet, and found his. She squeezed his hand and began to pump back and forth against him as they lay in a spoon-like back-to-belly position on their sides.

If she wanted to do the work, well, Longarm wasn't going to object. He lay still and let her enjoy herself.

Her strokes were short and strong, and she kept him deep inside her body there.

"Mm-mmm," she breathed. "Whew!"

"Um-hmm," he agreed.

She continued moving her ass. Stroking in and out. Longer strokes now and quicker.

He could hear her breath quicken and become ragged as the pleasure inside her built.

Longarm could feel the climb of it too. It gathered deep inside his balls and expanded. Filling him. Soon there would be too much feeling to contain, and it would spill outward.

Lenore grabbed at the sheet and pushed her face into the pillow as she muffled the screams and squeals of her release into the night silence around them.

Longarm could feel the convulsions rock and shudder through her body. He threw an arm over her waist and pressed the flat of his hand against her belly, drawing her to him and holding her close as he plunged and reared and speared himself deep inside her and his own pleasure exploded into her.

He gasped at the intense power of the release. From this angle the underside of his cock was pushed hard against the inside of Lenore's pelvic bones. The effect of that was to slow the flow of his climax and extend the pleasure of it for an impossibly long time.

109

He grunted and yanked her hard against him as the last drops spewed outward.

Lenore shuddered again and squeezed his hand hard.

"Thank you," she whispered in a hoarse, shaky voice. "Thank you, dear. I . . . I didn't know you still cared about me in . . . that way. It's been so long, dear."

Longarm frowned.

"I love you, darling," she whispered. She sounded like she was crying now. "I've always loved you. And I thought . . . I thought . . . because of those other women, you see . . . I thought . . . oh, darling, I'm so glad you've come back to my love. I'm so happy now, my darling Ben."

Ben?

Longarm felt cold.

His limp, spent prick was still lying there inside the heat of this woman's body.

And he hadn't any idea in the damned world who it was he'd just climbed into bed with and thoroughly fucked.

Chapter 23

All right. So what's a man supposed to do? Say, Oops, excuse me, lady, but I've made a little mistake?

Introduce himself, maybe?

Longarm groaned. This was embarrassing.

He felt himself shrivel up and become small. The contraction of his suddenly limp flesh pulled his cock out of her with a wet plop so that he was lying with it caught between her thighs instead of being inside her pussy.

Was that a more gentlemanly posture for a man to adopt with a woman he'd never met? Or should he have left it where it was?

The etiquette involved here wasn't something he'd given any great deal of thought to in the recent past.

The woman, whoever the hell she was, sighed and giggled and reached down between her legs to find him again.

She touched and fondled the wet, sticky flesh of him, and in spite of everything Longarm felt a surge of response to her manipulations.

He began to get hard again.

The woman wriggled backward against him, guiding him with her hands so that once more he entered her.

But this time not because he wanted to.

It would've been rude to jump up and run like hell, wouldn't it? Besides, his clothes and identification would give him away. Otherwise he might've tried it.

"Again, dear? Do you mind? I'd forgotten how wonderful it feels when you are inside me, dear."

She pushed her ass against him, trapping him deep inside her body, and found his hand to give it another squeeze.

Longarm stroked her hip and wondered how in hell he

had ever mistaken this woman for Lenore anyway.

Whoever this woman was, she was slimmer than chunky little Lenore and had a much-better-defined waist and a smaller, rounder ass.

She took his hand and pulled it around to her chest, and he discovered that she had nicer tits than Lenore did too. These were large and soft. Her nipples were hard protrusions against his palm. He rubbed and played with them as she obviously wanted, and the woman moaned and impaled herself on him with short, choppy, abrupt little strokes.

"You feel even better than I remembered, dear. Bigger and nicer, somehow." She sighed happily as Longarm squeezed her tits and rubbed her belly and went north again to tickle and tease her nipples.

That first time had been an honest mistake. He couldn't claim such an excuse this time.

He wished to hell there was some light in the room so he could get a look and see who or what it was he was in bed with.

No, he didn't, he decided quickly.

He didn't want to know.

Or did he?

"Don't pull out, dear, but could you roll on top of me now, please? I'd like to feel your weight on me. Just like this will be fine. I don't want to lose having you in me. Not even for a second."

Longarm pressed his belly tight against her butt and rolled on top of her. She lay face down with her legs parted. Her ass pushed hard against his stomach, but her pussy was hot and receptive.

He nuzzled the back of her neck and reached under her to find her tit again and squeeze it while he rode her from behind.

He could feel the slow, soft, trembling pulsations begin in her body and ripple through her frame.

She gasped and stiffened, once again burying her face in the pillow to stifle her cries.

Longarm increased the speed of his pounding. He drove himself hard onto her. Filled her. Took her. Spilled his seed into her.

He shuddered and stiffened in the spasms of release, then lowered his weight gently onto her back.

"Thank you," she said.

Longarm felt like a sonuvabitch.

It wasn't right to go on deceiving her.

But how the hell was he going to convince her now that . . . that what? He hadn't meant to? Of course he'd meant to. They'd both meant to. The difference was that she thought he was Ben. He was the only one who knew better. This time.

He groaned.

"You're wonderful," she whispered.

"Mmmm." He stroked her hair and the back of her neck.

"Did you enjoy it too?"

"Mm."

She sighed. "Kiss me, please?"

Oh, shit! He didn't see how that could work. If they got nose to nose and lip to lip there wasn't any way he could keep her from noticing this little error.

She laughed. "Never mind, dear. I don't feel like moving yet either."

"Mm."

"No, don't take it away yet. Leave it there, please. It feels so nice there."

"Mm."

He'd had it in mind that maybe he could slip over to the other side of the bed and wait for her to go back to sleep. Then he could gather up his things and sneak out. She might never even know. Hell, ol' Ben might even be the beneficiary of some loving attention in nights yet to come.

But it would be kinda hard to sneak away if he was still lying inside her like she wanted.

Dammit.

She found his hand and squeezed it and laughed again.

"I'm being quite awful to you, aren't I?"

"Mm?"

"Pretending like this, I mean."

"Mm?"

"Would you please stop that? I understand, dear, that you

113

don't want me to hear your voice, but that mumbling is wearisome."

"Oh," he said. He tried to move, but she took his hand and shook her head.

"Please don't. I do like feeling you there. If you don't mind, that is."

"You, uh . . ."

"Not at first," she admitted. "I really did think you were my husband the first time. But when you got on top of me . . . my Ben is an old dear, but he has much too much tummy for his own good. From behind like that he couldn't have gotten more than a few inches in."

"You, uh . . ."

"Mad? No. I suppose I should be. But I'm not. The truth is, dear, I liked it. Was it an honest mistake?"

"Yes. One of us must be in the wrong room, ma'am . . . that sounds strange, don't it? Calling you ma'am when we're like this? Anyhow, I thought you were somebody else. I wouldn't have . . ."

"I understand. In a way I suppose I'm glad. I've never been unfaithful to my husband. This way both of us have the excuse of honest error. The excuse but the pleasures too. Having our cake and eating it too."

"And they say it can't be done," he said with a smile.

"Which goes to show what 'they' don't know." She sighed and squeezed his hand and turned her shoulders, indicating that now he could roll off her back. "Oh, my, I do hate to feel that lovely thing leave me. But of course it must now that we've discovered our honest error, don't you think?"

"I'm afraid we prob'ly should. Although if you want—"

"No," she said quickly. "The next time would be no mistake, it would be infidelity."

"Of course," he said apologetically.

"Please leave me now, dear. Whoever you are." She laughed. "Don't tell me your name and don't let me see your face, dear. And I'll not tell you mine nor show myself to you. Besides, you would only be disappointed."

"I can't believe—"

"Hush. Thank you, but hush. You are a fine and hand-

114

some young soldier, no doubt, and I am probably old enough to be your mother, dear. I wouldn't want to disillusion you. And I certainly wouldn't want to ruin all the lovely fantasies I shall have in the future when I look at a strong young man and wonder if he is my fondly remembered visitor of the night. Go now. Please."

Longarm paused long enough to stroke her hair again and run his hands gently over her for a moment. "Close your eyes, please."

"All right, they're closed."

He bent down, cupped her chin in his palm, and pulled her face around so he could kiss her softly on the mouth. He couldn't see her in the dark. But he wished he could. He knew he would be looking at women he didn't know and wondering, for some time to come now.

"Good night," he whispered.

"Yes. Good night. So much nicer than good-bye."

He left the bed, silently gathered up his things, and carried them out to the sitting room to dress there.

He still had no idea which of them had made the mistake about the assigned quarters, but that was a problem he could detour by simply spending the rest of the night sleeping in a rocker on the post headquarters porch.

Longarm let himself out of the BOQ—or at least out of what he thought was the BOQ, the damn buildings all looked the same in the dark—and whistled softly as he walked across the compound toward the brick headquarters building.

Chapter 24

He found Moses Barnett at the warehouses working. Despite his age and experience the man was a common laborer, engaged when Longarm located him in carrying linen-wrapped slabs of smoked bacon from warehouse storage to a freight wagon scheduled to depart later in the day for the garrison at Fort Defiance in Arizona Territory.

"Can't talk to you now, mister. I'd get in trouble."

"You'll only get in trouble if you don't talk to me," Longarm told him. "Ask the sergeant if you like."

"I'll just do that, mister." Barnett dropped two sides of bacon into the back of the huge wagon and went inside. He was back a moment later with his gloves off and a slightly awed expression on his face. Longarm wasn't amazed. Aside from the already demonstrated eagerness from on high to assist in Longarm's investigation here, the sergeant in charge of this detail was the same man who'd been involved in the fracas with the pickpocket last night. The sergeant too was inclined to favor Deputy Long today.

"He said I'm t' take whatever time you want, suh, an' I won't even be docked pay for the time off."

Longarm smiled and led Barnett to a shady seat on a nearby loading platform.

"How can I help you, suh? Reckon I already told you 'bout all I know 'bout that battle an' the Mounted Volunteers."

"There are just a few more things I need to check with you, Moses. I recall you saying the Volunteers were issued carbines, but were there other arms issued as well?"

"I don't know what you mean, suh."

"Pistols, Moses. Or more accurately, revolvers. Were the

116

Mounted Volunteers issued revolvers before you set off on the campaign to Colorado?"

"Oh." Barnett shrugged. "Sure. We wanted sabers, see,'cuz that's what the dragoons had. We called mounted troops dragoons then, not calvary like they do now."

"Cavalry," Longarm corrected. Calvary was something quite different from cavalry.

"Right, calvary. What I'm telling you is that we thought of ourselves as dragoons in those days, not calvary. An' dragoons carried pretty sabers. All us boys wanted sabers but they give us revolving pistols instead."

"Old Colt pistols, Moses?"

"No, suh, not that I ever seen. General Sibley, he was a man liked t' do things right. He bought us a shipment o' bran'-new Griswold an' Grier revolving pistols, suh. Latest thing they was then, though they wouldn't seem like it t'day, them bein' cap-an'-ball pistols an' not the cat'ridge guns the troops all carry now. But at the time, see, they was first class. Looked like Colt pistols, mind, but they wasn't. They was made . . . I dunno. N' Orleans, Mobile, someplace like that. Not made by damnyankees anyhow. We wasn't buying anything outa the Northern factories by then. Couldn't. We was under what you call a blockade. There was lots of stuff you couldn't buy then 'cuz of that."

Longarm frowned.

He'd been so *sure* that the Paterson Colt played a part in this somewhere.

It all seemed to be linked together. The people linked then to Sibley's invasion of New Mexico and the Paterson Colt linked now somehow with the people.

Damn it.

He'd been hoping . . . hell, he didn't know what he'd been hoping for. Something. Anything. He pulled out a cheroot and lit it, pondering as he occupied himself with the routine of getting the slim cigar lit.

"The other day, Moses, you said you remember Major Frazier from that campaign. I want you to see if you can recall a couple more names too. Tom Jepp?"

"Sar'nt Jepp? 'Course I remember him. Sar'nt Jepp was practically famous. He used t' be a Ranger before the war,

117

you know. Played hell all along the border chasing Mex'can raiders was what we heard. Came the conflict Sar'nt Jepp coulda stayed on the border, but he resigned from the Rangers an' enlisted with the Volunteers. The major—or maybe it was somebody else, I wouldn't be knowing—made him a sar'nt right off. Sar'nt Jepp was in charge o' a lot o' the training we had 'fore we rode out. Not that there was so much of it, mind, but they done what they could. Sar'nt Jepp told us how t' act when the bullets started flying, an' he was right 'bout everything he said too. Then later, once we got up into New Mexico here, the sar'nt was attached t' the headquarters squad. Don't know for sure what he done, but he was always close t' the officers at the front o' the column. He was an awful good man, Sar'nt Jepp."

"Do you remember seeing Sergeant Jepp at the Apache Canyon fight?" Longarm asked.

Barnett rubbed at his chin, turned his head, and spat a stream of yellow tobacco juice at a beetle that was laboring across the timbers of the loading dock.

"Ayuh, I b'lieve maybe I do. Yeah, I b'lieve he was there that day. Him and the major too. They was trying to rally some o' the boys to protect the baggage mules. Got a few t'gether, I think, but I don't know whatever became of none of those fellows. The bunch I was with, we got cut off from them by a squadron o' them screaming sons o' bitches from Colorado, and I b'lieve that's the last I ever saw of Sar'nt Jepp or the major, either one."

"Jepp wasn't with you on the retr . . . on the march back home to Texas?"

"No, suh, I don't recall seein' him after that Apache Canyon fight. He wasn't with my bunch that time. But then o' course we was all scattered and split apart after Glorietta. That's what they call it now, y'know. The Battle o' Glorietta Pass. Like it was all one fight, Glorietta an' Apache Canyon an' that ranch in another o' the canyons. I wasn't there an' forget what the name o' that place was, but I remember hearing there was more fighting there. Some ranch. I dunno. All I seen was the ambush in Glorietta Pass an' then later the attacks on the supply trains in Apache Canyon. The other stuff, well, I just don't know. It was

118

all dust an' shooting an' running like hell. That's mostly what I recall of it."

That part of the three-pronged battle, Longarm thought he remembered hearing, had taken place on a ranch owned by a family named Pigeon. Not that it made any difference now if Frazier, Jepp, and Barnett hadn't been there.

"Thank you, Moses. Does the name Caswell mean anything to you from those days?"

"Caswell? Sure. Casey, his first name was. Corporal Caswell." Barnett rolled his eyes and whistled. "Mean son of a bitch too."

"Oh?"

"Yes, suh. Nobody wanted to get Corporal Caswell mad at 'em. Nobody. He like to've kilt one man that stole a jar o' boot black off him before we left San Antone. Dumb son of a bitch sure didn't know it was the corporal's boot black he was lifting or he'd've left it alone, let me tell you. Corporal caught that fella in the act, see, an' snatched up the first thing he grabbed hold of, which happened t' be a coat tree, an' laid it plumb across the fella's head. Busted the coat tree an' the man's head too. The fella wasn't fit t' ride or fight after that an' had t' be sent home from the army." Barnett chuckled. "I seen that man after the war, Marshal. He stayed at home there an' got rich buyin' and sellin' foreign-made stuff. Dealt across the border, see, where there wasn't no blockade an' them foreign ships could put in t' port. That fella stayed home an' got rich while the rest of us boys rode off t' war an' got shot at. Makes you think, don't it?"

"You were telling me about Caswell," Longarm reminded him.

"The corporal. Right. Mean, like I said. An' about the brownest-nosed suck-ass you ever seen. Corporal Caswell was always hangin' on to Sar'nt Jepp's coattails or else sucking up t' one o' the officers if there was one o' them handy. I never liked Corporal Caswell. I don't think none o' the boys did."

"Was he in the Apache Canyon fight too?"

"Had t' be, Marshal. Wherever Sar'nt Jepp an' them officers went, Corporal Caswell was right behind 'em with

119

his nose stuck in the crack o' the highest-ranking one's ass. You could count on that. But don't get me wrong. That sonuvabitch could fight. He was a suck-ass, but he wasn't no coward. When those Coloradans jumped us in the pass an' came charging down over us, I seen Corporal Caswell take two of 'em on with an empty carbine. Busted the stock o' his gun over one of 'em's heads an' stabbed the other in the eyes with the splintered end of it. That man warn't no coward, whatever else he mighta been."

Damn! Longarm thought.

The murdered men all *were* tied tight together in that long ago battle.

"When you think of those three men, Moses, Major Frazier and Sergeant Jepp and Corporal Caswell, who else comes to mind? Who else might have been close to them or ridden with them a lot back then?"

"Oh hell, I dunno, Marshal. Lot's o' fellas in that outfit, you know."

"But were there any in particular that you might think of in connection with those three I've already named to you?"

Barnett shrugged. "The lieutenants, maybe. The captain, he kinda stayed to himself mostly. But both the lieutenants was close t' the major, an' Sar'nt Jepp was too, an' Corporal Caswell was close t' whoever he thought might do him some good."

"Who were the lieutenants, Moses?"

"Lemme see now. There was Lieutenant Abramson. He was a pretty good officer. He got killed by them Coloradans sometime in that fighting, but I don't recall was it in Glorietta or Apache. Then there was Lieutenant Brice. I never heard what happened to him."

"Brice. Do you remember his first name, Moses?"

Barnett grinned. "Sure, Marshal. Far as I was concerned, his first name was Lieutenant."

Longarm smiled. "Is there anyone else, Moses? It doesn't necessarily have to be an officer or a non-com. Were there any private soldiers who hung around with Frazier and Jepp and Caswell?"

"The bugler, maybe. He was just a kid. Buddy, he was called. I don't remember what his proper name was. Everybody just called him Buddy. Wherever the major went, the bugler did too, o'course."

"Anyone else?"

Longarm continued to prod at Moses Barnett, but it was like taking your tongue to a sore tooth. It was something you just naturally did, but it didn't accomplish anything.

A lieutenant in the Mounted Volunteers named Brice and a young bugler with the nickname Buddy.

If these murders tied in somehow with a half-forgotten battle in a backwater of that long-ended war, one of those men could be the killer Longarm was looking for today.

And one of them could hold the key to why a revolving pistol that had been an obsolete antique even back then was suddenly so fascinating to the Confederate veterans today.

Longarm thanked Moses Barnett and walked across the compound toward the message center. By now he should have some answers to the telegrams he'd sent out earlier.

He certainly hoped he did, because he was coming up awfully short when he tried to work out answers for himself.

Chapter 25

The message center had messages, all right. Pages of 'em. If the day operator looked at Longarm now with a certain amount of hidden loathing, Longarm couldn't much blame the man. It must have taken hours to receive all of this. Some bureaucratic clerk in some dusty Austin cubbyhole had been busy.

There were reports on former Ranger Tom Jepp. Former Lieutenant Ralph Frazier, U.S.A., later Major Ralph Frazier, C.S.A. And a brief mention too of K. C. Caswell.

Longarm put all of those on the bottom of the pile, though, and turned first to the wire from Denver that had been interrupted during transmission the other day.

He scanned it quickly, then smiled.

Good old Henry. Billy Vail's clerk understood Longarm's concern for the boss and had sent along reassuring word, and damn the extra expense on the government ledgers.

Mrs. Vail was all right. She had something, unspecified, that a simple application of powders would cure. Billy had to be feeling better now. Longarm was glad for Billy's sake and for his lady's.

As for the work at hand, Henry relayed Billy's instruction that Longarm was to continue pursuit of former Ranger Jepp on charges of interfering with the duties of a federal officer.

Longarm frowned and reflected. He hadn't gotten around to mentioning to anybody in Denver yet that Tom Jepp was as dead as Caswell now.

It was a simple enough oversight.

And one that Longarm didn't figure to correct quite yet.

It'd be stretching the point to ask the marshal to extend Longarm's jurisdiction to include whoever murdered Jepp.

Whoever did that had committed a crime that was against territorial law, not federal.

But dammit, Longarm had this one under his skin now. He plain and simple wanted to keep on with it.

Jurisdiction could be worked out afterward.

And if Billy didn't know . . .

"I'll want to send a few more wires please, Corporal," Longarm told the telegraph operator.

Give the guy credit. If he was groaning, he at least had the good grace to keep it under his breath so Longarm couldn't hear.

Longarm dispatched messages to Austin again, informing the Ranger headquarters of Jepp's murder and asking this time for all available information on a former Mounted Volunteer lieutenant named Brice and on a company-level bugler with the name or nickname of Buddy.

The telegraph operator quivered a little when he read those requests, but he didn't say anything.

"You'll be waiting here for the answers, Marshal?"

Longarm thought for a moment before he answered. The quick and obvious solution would be for the Fort Union message center to receive the answers whenever they came in and then relay them to Longarm wherever he happened to be.

But considering the heft of the voluminous responses already in hand, that would be playing a dirty one indeed on the message-center boys here if these new answers were even half so comprehensive as the first ones. It would make the operator take down all of it once and then have to turn around and send it all out again to wherever Longarm found himself.

"If I don't wait on post," Longarm told the man, "I'll have you send a courier to me."

The corporal looked mighty relieved. He very nearly smiled.

"I'll let you know where to find me," Longarm told him, then picked up the thick sheaf of information already received from Austin and carried it outside. He headed toward the officers' mess, figuring he could find something to eat there and read at the same time.

• • •

Longarm dismounted and tied the sturdy bay horse to a public hitching rail outside City Hall. He found Police Chief Carl Worley in his office filling out forms.

"Well?" Worley demanded as soon as Longarm came in.

Longarm shrugged and dropped the pile of reports onto Worley's desk to join all the other papers already there.

"Nothing I hadn't already learned from Barnett, I'm afraid. But there's the connection, Carl. All three of the dead men were members of the same unit in the Mounted Volunteers under Sibley. All three of 'em knew each other pretty good then. All three of 'em fought at Santa Fe and Glorietta and lastly in Apache Canyon. Only Tom Jepp shows any official C.S.A. service record after that date. Jepp mustered out at Austin in '65 and rejoined the Rangers. That didn't last long, of course. There's a gap in his record from the time the Rangers was disbanded by the Reconstruction government until they were formed again. When the state allowed the Ranger service back into operation, Tom Jepp was one of the first men signed.

"As for the other two, Frazier and Caswell both were presumed dead after the Battle of Glorietta Pass. Which we know ain't true, but those records don't. Neither man is listed on any company rolls after Apache Canyon."

Worley grunted. "They were out of circulation a long time," he said. "Frazier living under an assumed name and Caswell in the Colorado territorial prison."

"Neither one of them ever left this part of the country, it looks like. Never went back to Texas at all, I'd guess. But why?"

"If we knew that, Longarm, we might know what's behind these murders."

Longarm frowned and helped himself to a chair. He crossed his legs, offered a cheroot to Carl Worley, and lit one for himself. "One little thing in those papers, Carl, tells me that the Fort Union adjutant's faith in Ralph Frazier might not've been well placed."

"Oh?"

"Little item on page five of the Frazier report. Right

toward the bottom there. It's an entry showing where a Mrs. Edith Frazier filed a death-benefits claim against the state of Texas asking for a war widow's pension. She was awarded fifteen dollars a month."

"So?"

"So Frazier was married when he disappeared, and let his wife believe he'd died. When he up and walked away from Trinidad the other day, it wasn't the first time he'd found it convenient to abandon a family. Kinda tells you something about the man's character, don't it? Respected and upstanding on the surface, but maybe with some dry rot underneath the bark, hmm?"

"And what we need to know, Longarm, is what else the man was up to. Him and the others."

"Uh, huh."

"Those three and probably someone else right here in Las Vegas."

"Any luck from your end, Carl?"

"Not so far. I have two locals gone on a fishing trip into the mountains and one businessman down in Santa Fe on a buying trip. His son is running the store while he's away. All three of the people who I know aren't in town right now, though, have talked about their plans for the past couple weeks or longer. Nobody's gone missing all of a sudden."

"How about locals who served under General Sibley at Glorietta Pass?"

"I've asked, but no luck so far. Don't forget, though, this area didn't have much in the way of an Anglo population until after the war. We have folks here who served both sides of the conflict. It's considered polite to not bring up old hurts. The men who were in uniform then tend not to talk about it now lest they get hard feelings stirred up with a neighbor who might've worn a different-color cap."

"No clubs or veterans' organizations or anything like that?"

"Not here, Longarm. But my people are still asking it around. We might learn something yet."

"Dammit, Carl, I was hoping . . ."

"Yeah." Worley pushed away from the desk and stood

up. "Why don't we have some dinner while we think on it."

Longarm grimaced. But he stood and joined the police chief. There didn't seem to be anything more productive they could accomplish until or unless they learned more.

Chapter 26

"Chief?"

Worley and Longarm both looked up from their supper plates. The man standing by the table was a slender young fellow dressed like a cowboy but wearing a badge pinned to his vest. He wasn't one of Worley's policemen, Longarm knew, because they were required to wear a copper-buttoned blue uniform coat and blue kepi.

"Yes, John?"

"Sorry to bother you, Chief, but Sheriff Montoya and his wife left this afternoon for Mora."

"I remember him saying they were going to go visit her sisters. John. What of it?"

"Well, I'm kinda in charge till the sheriff gets back, Chief. And the truth is, sir, I'd like your help with something that come up just now. I'd, well, I'd hate to do something to mess it up, sir. I've never worked a murder case before."

"Murder?"

"Yes, sir. Out at the Budde ranch. I know that's outside your jurisdiction, sir, but . . ."

"Of course I'll come, John." Worley dropped his napkin onto the table and stood. "Do you want to join us, Longarm?"

"Sure."

Longarm stood also, and Worley performed the introductions. The young sheriff's deputy was John White. He seemed relieved to have the help of both the Las Vegas police chief and a deputy U.S. marshal with his first murder investigation.

It took a few minutes to gather horses for the unexpected trip out of town. Then the three officers from three entirely separate jurisdictions rode east from Las Vegas. They forded the shallow Gallinas fork of the Pecos and rode on into the night.

Longarm hung back and let Carl Worley take charge at the ranch house. The police chief seemed to know what he was doing. He struck a match to light the way, and was careful to avoid disturbing anything in the house as he found a lamp and lit it.

While he was doing that John White was talking to the handful of Mexican *vaqueros* who were assembled in the yard. The young deputy's Spanish came out in a slow drawl, but seemed fluid and fluent to Longarm's untrained ear. Facility with languages was something that Longarm admired and mildly envied.

"You can come in now if you want," Worley said when he had the room lit.

Longarm left White and the *vaqueros* to their unfathomable conversation and went in.

It was a murder scene, all right.

From the doorway he could now see a huge blood puddle on the hardwood floor, and more blood on the back wall and the boots and lower legs of a body that lay behind an overstuffed armchair in the front room.

Unless somebody'd taken to using the ranch house to slaughter a steer, the man on the floor had to be dead. No one body could lose that much blood and survive. In fact, it was fairly amazing that that much blood could come out of one human body. There was an awful lot of it. It would have looked like even more before it dried.

"Son of a bitch," Worley exclaimed as Longarm came in.

"What?"

"This isn't either one of the Budde brothers."

"Oh?"

"This is Tyrone Day. I bought some tobacco off Ty just this morning."

"In town, that'd be."

"Of course. Ty runs—ran, I suppose I should say now—a store just down the street from City Hall. Hell, Longarm,

128

he's been in Las Vegas even longer than I have. He was one of the first men I met when I came here." Worley shook his head and moved around to view his friend's body from another angle.

"Not much question what killed him," Longarm observed.

"Not much," Worley agreed.

The dead man's chest had been torn apart by a shotgun blast at close range. Both barrels, was Longarm's guess. The amount of damage was incredible.

Worley knelt and laid his fingertips against the side of Day's neck, then lifted one arm and worked the wrist back and forth.

"Cool," he said, "but not long enough to stiffen up. This afternoon some time, I'd say. You agree?"

Longarm bent down and made the same crude tests. "Yeah, I'd say so."

"Damn. Look how the man's dressed here."

Longarm shrugged. There was nothing exceptional about Day's clothes. Boots, jeans, flannel shirt . . . what was left of it now . . . and an ancient and battered black slouch hat. He wore a gunbelt and black holster, a castoff military type with a retaining flap that covered the entire butt of the revolver. That style was protective of the gun and a sensible design for anyone who wasn't interested in fast draws or fancy gunplay. Longarm would have preferred it himself if he'd been in a different line of work.

As for the man who was wearing those clothes, Day was middle-aged or a bit more and had a paunch. His hands were soft from years of working behind a store counter. Wire-rimmed spectacles sat askew on his pale face.

"I don't see nothing unusual, Carl," he admitted.

"Well, I sure as hell do, Longarm. All the years I've known Ty I've never seen him with a pair of boots or a hat like this. And I've never known him to touch a gun except to take one off a shelf and hand it to a customer. He's always worn low-cut shoes and broadcloth trousers. Only wore a hat on Sundays, and then it was always a derby. Ty wasn't one to get out hunting or fishing or riding horseback. Never. He was real quiet. Didn't drink with the boys or carouse much. He'd visit the whorehouse Saturday nights, and that's about it. Nice fella. So what's he doing dressed like this an' lying dead in Bud's place?"

Longarm grunted. He had no other answer to give. Fortunately this wasn't his case to have to worry about, though.

John White came inside to join them. Longarm could see the worried-looking *vaqueros* hanging around near the porch steps.

"I told them you might want to talk to them too, Chief."

"All right."

White came over beside the body, looked down, and went pale. Longarm could see his throat flutter and clench as he gagged and tried to hold it back. Sweat beaded his forehead, but he got control of himself and kept from puking. If this wasn't the young deputy's first body, Longarm realized, it was at least his first messy one.

"Hey, Chief, that isn't Bud; it's Mr. Day," White said as soon as he could manage the words.

"Sure is, John."

"Julio . . . he's the one found the body and sent for the sheriff . . . he said it was Bud."

"Did he come inside?"

"No, sir. He said the hands were all out riding bog today while Bud and Tony stayed here at the place. When they got in, Julio came to the house to report in on what they done today. It was near dark but not quite by then, he said. He knocked on the door and didn't get no answer, so he poked his head inside to call out to them. That's when he seen the body and thought it was Bud. Because of the boots, I'd guess. Tony always wears those tan-colored ones. Julio says he could see Bud was dead, and none of the hands wanted to come inside with a dead man here."

Longarm frowned. "We haven't looked in any of the other rooms," he suggested.

"Shit, Bud and Tony might be lying dead in the house too," Worley said.

Each of the men grabbed a lamp and went to check through the rest of the house.

130

Chapter 27

"So where the hell are Bud and Tony?" Worley complained as he lowered himself into a chair. Tyrone Day's body lay a few feet away with a sheet draped over it.

"Julio says they were supposed to be here," White said. "Neither one of them said anything about going anywhere when they sent the hands off to work this morning."

"They sure as hell aren't here now. On the surface of things it looks like one or both of them shot Day, then realized there wasn't any way they could hide it and took off running."

"I'll get Julio and take him out to the barn with me, Chief. He can tell us if there's horses missing."

"Good idea, John."

The sheriff's deputy left, and Longarm pulled a cheroot out and lit it.

"These Budde brothers," Longarm said. "Did they have any feud going with Day?"

"Not that I heard about, and I promise you I would have heard if there were any words between them. Hell, Bud and Tony traded at Ty's store in town. They always seemed to get along real good. If there was bad blood there, it came up after Ty came out here today. And I still don't understand him doing that, especially dressed like he is now."

"How old are the Buddes, Carl?"

"Oh, about Ty's age, I'd guess. Tony is anyhow. Bud's the younger of the two by eight or nine years. Easier to get to know too. Bud's the talkative one. Tony is quiet, kind of like Ty Day was."

Longarm grunted. "You mind if I look around? I'd kinda like to poke into the dresser drawers and like that."

"Help yourself. You have an idea about something, Long-arm?"

"Not really. Just a notion."

Worley stayed where he was while Longarm took a lamp back into the nearer bedroom and began searching for clues that probably didn't exist.

"I'll be a son of a bitch," Worley said.

"Possible connection with the other killings?" Longarm asked.

"Damn sure could be," the Las Vegas police chief agreed.

Both men were looking at a tarnished brass bugle that Longarm had unearthed from a trunk in the bedroom Julio said was used by the younger brother Bud.

"Budde. Buddy. This guy could be the Mounted Volunteer bugler Moses Barnett mentioned."

"And Tony?"

"Damned if I'd know. Barnett never said if his Buddy had a brother enlisted in the same outfit. But then maybe he wouldn't have known. He wasn't close to the people at the top, and the boys involved in this all seem to have been in that category. Officers and senior non-coms."

"For that matter," Worley said, "maybe they weren't actually brothers. Just partnered together and pretended to be. They don't look much alike. But then when two fellas tell you they're brothers, you just naturally figure that's what they are."

"And Day?" Longarm asked.

"He never talked about being in the war. But like I told you already, that doesn't mean much around here. He's the right age for it. Most men in our age range served under one flag or the other." The chief volunteered no information about his own service, although he too probably had worn one color uniform or the other a few years back. Longarm understood; he had the same habit of reticence himself.

Longarm stood and went over to the body under the sheet. He pulled the covering back a few inches and picked up the slouch hat the corpse had been wearing.

"It's dusty and it's old, but shape the crown a little differ-

132

ent and it's an old Kossuth," Longarm said. "It could've been an issue hat."

"For either side," Worley said. During the early days of the war, both armies had purchased hats, swords, and certain other small pieces of equipment from the same suppliers in England and Europe. And Southern units were often outfitted from supplies taken when the Union forts on Southern territory were captured early in the scrap. Several forts had been taken in Texas, in particular, and their stores commandeered by the Confederate forces. On the other hand, after the war the Kossuth service hats had been dumped onto the surplus market by the hundreds of thousands and resold for pennies. They had been worn by miners, cowboys, and just plain laborers from one coast to the other. They were still seen on the streets fairly often.

"Day could have known the Budde brothers during the war," Longarm said. "Is it reaching to think he might have known the rest of them too?"

"Damned if I know."

"Could Day ride a horse?"

"I never saw him do it, but about anybody can sit on a saddle," Worley said.

"Yet he chose to come out here in a heavy wagon," Longarm said. The head *vaquero*, Julio, said the wagon parked beside the barn and the four-up of heavy horses now standing in the corral didn't belong on the ranch. The Budde brothers' personal horses and saddles were gone, but Julio had never seen the wagon before he and White went to look in the barn.

"The wagon isn't Ty's," Worley said. "It looks like the rig Schaumauer owns. I have no idea what Ty Day would have been doing with it. I've never known Schaumauer to loan it to anybody."

"Another puzzle with no easy answer," Longarm said.

"I got to say, Longarm. Things have gotten exciting since you came around."

"It wasn't hardly intentional, Carl."

"If I thought it was, man, I'd come over there and punch you square in the mouth."

Longarm smiled. He knew what the police chief meant.

Trouble is a peace officer's job, but certainly not his preference.

"I suppose we'd best go back to town," Worley said. He sounded tired. "I'll put wires out to get the hunt started for Bud and Tony."

"What do you want me t' do, Chief?" Deputy White asked.

"You're in charge of the investigation until the sheriff gets back, John, so you do what you think best. If it was me, I think I'd stay here tonight, and come morning see if those *vaqueros* couldn't help me start tracking the Budde brothers."

"All right. Will it be okay if I send the body to town now? One of the *vaqueros* can load it into that wagon and drive it in. It's gonna need tending to pretty soon."

"That's a good idea, John. Meantime Longarm and me will start in. I don't want to have to keep pace with that heavy old thing or those boys will get clean out of the country before I can get the warnings out on them."

"Any time you're ready, Carl." Longarm stood and turned to the young deputy. "You're doing just fine with this, John. We'll make sure the sheriff knows that when he gets back."

"Thanks," White said with obvious relief. "Thanks for the help too. Both of you."

Longarm glanced at the stars when he and Worley stepped out onto the porch. It was the middle of the night already and would be considerably later by the time they got back to Las Vegas.

And every minute of that passing time gave the Budde brothers that much greater a lead on the search that was being launched for them.

There was no actual proof, Longarm realized, that this murder and the ones he was following were tied into the same sequence.

But Longarm had a gut feeling that they were.

Finding the Budde brothers might prove that one way or the other.

Chapter 28

Longarm grunted with satisfaction after he picked up the messages waiting for him at the Las Vegas telegraph office. The unknown clerk in distant Austin had come through for him again.

There had been a C.S.A. second lieutenant named Anthony Brice assigned to the Mounted Volunteer company commanded by Major Ralph Frazier, C.S.A. And the company bugler's name was Jason Budde.

Longarm figured he'd found the Budde "brothers" and their past.

He shot another wire off to Austin asking about the possible service record of a man named Tyrone Day—that helpful clerk was gonna learn to hate Custis Long before this one was ended—and carried the messages already in hand over to City Hall to share the information with Chief Worley.

"Chief's over at Ty Day's place," the policeman on desk duty told Longarm. "You know where that is?"

Longarm got directions and went back out onto the street. Day's residence was on the second floor of his shop building, a few minutes walk away. Longarm stretched his legs getting there.

"Good morning, Longarm."

"Mornin', Carl. You finding anything?" The police chief and another officer were going through Day's things piece by piece.

"Enough to tell us for sure that Ty was a Confederate." Worley motioned toward a small collection of memorabilia that he'd found and piled on top of the dead shopkeeper's dressing table. There were a few brass buttons, a C.S.A. belt buckle, faded yellow sergeant's chevrons, and a wind-beaten silk guidon with tattered fringe that had been folded carefully and protected with care inside a leather case.

"Color guard," Longarm suggested.

"Uh, huh," Worley agreed.

"Another insider at the top of the heap. Color guards and buglers consort with the mucky-mucks."

"Uh, huh."

"It's more than a pattern, it's a fact," Longarm said.

"But what the hell does it *mean*?" Worley complained.

"Damn, Carl, I was depending on you to tell me."

Worley smiled and went back to his search of Tyrone Day's things. "By the way," he said over his shoulder, "I talked to Hans Schaumauer this morning."

"The guy who owns that wagon?"

"The guy who used to own that wagon," Worley corrected. "Hans said Ty bought the rig off him yesterday forenoon. Hans hadn't had any thought of selling it, but Ty came in off the street and made him a cash offer on the spot. Twice what the wagon and team were worth. Hans liked those horses awful well, but—"

"But for double what they were worth he was willing to kiss them good-bye," Longarm said, finishing the sentence for him.

"Right."

"I don't suppose Mr. Day said anything to the gentleman about why he had to have a big rig and four-up that bad all of a sudden."

"Very carefully didn't give a reason, Hans says. In fact, he tells me Ty was nervous and acted kinda secretive. Which wasn't like Ty Day at all. The man was always quiet, like I told you, but I've never known him to be a nervous sort, and he sure was never secretive about anything. Schaumauer thought it was awfully odd too." Worley turned his head to give Longarm a wink and a smug smile. "But I haven't told you the most interesting part of the transaction."

"Oh?"

"Hans says Ty paid him in gold."

Longarm frowned and shrugged. "So?" In this country damn few men trusted paper currency. The counterfeiters had gone to the well too often for most folks to trust printed money. And gold coin was simply more convenient to carry than a comparable value in silver.

"Ty paid for the wagon and team in gold pesos, Longarm. *Spanish* gold pesos. We see Mexican money around here fairly often. But personally I'd never seen any Spanish gold coin. Not ever." The police chief went over to Tyrone Day's wardrobe and took a leather-covered and very handsome box or small chest out of it. He opened it and handed it to Longarm.

The velvet lining inside the empty box held faint, circular impressions where something the approximate size and shape of twenty-peso gold coins must have lain for a very long time.

"Looks like Mr. Day had a stash that he hadn't dipped into all these years," Longarm said.

"Until yesterday," Worley agreed.

"Until something came up that was so important he was willing to abandon his business, grab his stash, and go," Longarm said.

"Sounds familiar, don't it," Worley observed.

"Yeah. Don't it just."

"And he felt he needed a large wagon and four horses to accomplish it. Except he managed to get himself killed before it happened for him."

Longarm grunted.

There was something . . . he couldn't quite nail it down and hold it still so he could look it over . . . there was something, some thought, tickling the back recesses of his mind. Something somebody'd said. Something somebody'd implied. Something Longarm hadn't paid enough damn attention to.

Whatever it was, dammit, consciously fretting about it wasn't going to drag it to the surface on demand.

Finding that kind of half-formed thought was like trying to see something in the dark. Instead of staring at it straight on you had to sneak up on it sideways and a bit at a time. A glimpse and then another, until finally it all materialized into one piece like one of those optical-illusion puzzles that were printed in magazines, the things that look like just so many dots and squiggles until you once see the hidden picture and then can't ever again figure out how you missed seeing it the first time.

This, he realized, was very much like that, and if he wanted to find out what it was he would just have to let it germinate in the back of his mind until it was ready to be seen. Then it would float to the surface to be studied.

"I don't know about you, Carl, but I haven't taken time for breakfast yet. Care to join me?"

"Sure." Worley told his officer to finish the search and let him and the federal deputy know if anything interesting turned up. Then the two peace officers went downstairs and out into the morning sunshine.

Chapter 29

Longarm finished his belated breakfast alone. The police chief had been called away to attend to a problem of major local concern. Something to do with two neighbors who got into a squabble over the first man's wife stealing her washday laundry water from a well and pump belonging to the second man. The wives had gotten into it first and dragged the husbands in behind them, and now Husband One had a black eye and Husband Two a broken nose and all four of them were shouting threats to sue each other.

Worley had given Longarm a wink and smile and gone off to pour oil onto the troubled waters.

That, Longarm reflected, was the sort of thing a federal officer didn't have to worry about. Thank goodness for small favors.

He lit a cheroot to enjoy while he finished his coffee, then ambled out onto the street.

He avoided the temptation to go back to the telegraph office and lean over the operator's shoulder waiting for something to come in. Something from Austin or, better, something from a neighboring town to say that Bud and Tony Budde had been picked up and were awaiting interrogation.

That would have been ideal. But it was unrealistic too.

And if Longarm was going to have to contain his impatience he might as well do it without disrupting anyone else's working day. He figured he owed the telegraph operators here and elsewhere at least that much consideration in light of all the work he was putting them through.

He wandered along the main business district of Las Vegas, stopping here to admire a pair of finely crafted boots and there to look at some new shirts. He bought some cheroots at another shop and picked up some matches to go with them. All in all he was having a thrillingly productive morning. And exercising his jaw quite a bit with all the yawning he was doing. He paid for his purchases and went back out onto the sidewalk.

"Why, Marshal Long. How nice to see you again."

He smiled and swept his Stetson off. "Miss Crane. Good morning to you."

Lenore glanced over her shoulder, but there was no one near to overhear. "I've looked for you the past several nights. Shame on you for not being there," she said in a considerably lower voice.

"Duty calls," he said with a smile. "Regrettable but true." He suspected that Lenore was the kind of girl who would find it amusing to learn that Longarm had tried to make love to her more recently than she knew. But then he just might be wrong about that too. Best to keep his mouth shut and not risk making the mistake, he decided.

"You look nice today," he added. It was true. She wasn't really that attractive a girl, but today she was making the most of what she had. She wore a frilly go-to-town dress and was carrying a parasol to shield her from the sun. Young ladies, after all, were much too delicate to have harsh sunlight strike them. They just might wilt.

"I could say as much about you, sir," she said in a normal voice, and then dropped it closer to a whisper to add, "But it isn't what you look like, dear, that I remember so well. Yum, yum."

"Yum?"

"Yum," she confirmed. "Could you wait here a moment?"

"Of course."

Lenore went back inside the shop she'd just emerged from. She was gone no more than a few seconds, then came back out onto the sidewalk.

"I told Mama I was going to take a stroll. We came in so she could look for a new hat—the Commandant's Ball is coming up next month, you see—and that will take almost forever."

"She won't mind me spiriting you away from her?"

"Heavens, no. Mama knows I don't enjoy shopping near-ly so much as she does. Besides, she always likes a little time alone when we come to town. That way she can buy her nerve medicine and we can both pretend that I don't know about it."

"Is she all right?" Longarm asked, the polite concern only skin-deep but nonetheless expected.

Lenore laughed. "Of course, silly. It's one of those patent medicines that's mostly alcohol. Mama would faint dead away if anyone suggested that she drank, but she has to have her half bottle of nerve medicine every evening. And this isn't the sort of thing that Papa would prescribe for her. I don't know how she manages it, but I really don't think he knows."

Longarm wasn't sure how to handle that particular brand of honesty, so he let the comment lie there and gracefully die. He trailed along beside Lenore as the girl twirled her parasol over her shoulder and walked in a seemingly aimless stroll through town.

"Do you know where we're going?" he asked after a few minutes.

"Um, hum," she said sweetly. But she didn't elaborate on it.

They chatted idly about events at the fort that Longarm didn't care about and people there who Longarm didn't know. Lenore seemed quite content.

And Longarm had no reason not to be either. After all, the day was fine and the girl's company pleasant.

"This way," she said. She turned off the street. The side-walks had long since disappeared behind them, and now they were approaching a nearly dry creek bed that was shaded by ancient, drooping cottonwoods and lined with thick stands of low willow. Longarm dutifully followed where Lenore led.

She glanced back behind them, but no one was paying attention. Lenore closed her parasol and used it like a prod to part the willows in front of her. She pushed through them, Longarm close behind, and came out onto the rim of a steep bank above the tiny creek.

The creek looked more like a ditch here, but upstream, to the west, there was a flat, grassy area. Lenore turned in that direction, humming softly under her breath.

They were surrounded by the willows and sheltered by the cottonwoods.

Even though there were houses not more than sixty yards distant and an entire town business district very little further away, the impression given by the surroundings was that they might have been in a wilderness setting miles and miles from civilization. The only things visible that would give that the lie were a few barely seen rooftops and a chimney or two.

Lenore smiled, still humming, and came into Longarm's arms. "You may kiss me now."

"Thank you," he said with a smile.

He did. Thoroughly. He could feel Lenore's knees sag, and her mouth on his was fevered and eager.

"I've always wanted to do it outdoors," she whispered into his mouth.

"Are you sure . . . ?"

"Hush up and undo me." She disengaged herself from him and turned, presenting her back to him so he could unfasten the three hundred or so tiny buttons there.

The girl was a bold little thing and no doubt about it.

But what the lady wanted . . .

He unfastened the interminably long row of miniature buttons. "You'd best hope I can get these miserable little things done up again without tearing half o' them off," he said.

Lenore laughed and wriggled her butt against his crotch.

"I swear, woman, it must take you two hours to get dressed in the morning." Once the back of the dress was open she hardly had a start on undressing. "Getting a lady out of all this junk is like peeling an onion. Except an onion doesn't have so many layers."

"Now the corset, please."

He untied and unlaced and tugged apart.

"Whew!" she said. "Thanks. At least now I can breathe again." Lenore just didn't have a figure that was intended to take on the shape that was required of proper young ladies, so a shape was artificially created for her. The experience must be a painful one, Longarm guessed.

Once the corset was out of the way it didn't take her long to get down to skin.

She stood naked in the sun-dappled shade and grinned at him. She looked young and impish and happy here. Prettier, really, than she had the other night.

"Now you," she prompted. "Unless you're too shy."

Longarm laughed and stripped. It was a much easier chore than hers had been.

Lenore looked at him and sighed. "Another dream fulfilled, um?"

"Glad to be of service, ma'am."

Lenore came into his arms again. Her skin was cool and soft against his hard body, but her mouth was hot and her tongue dartingly quick.

He picked her up and carried her a few feet west along the creek bank to a bed of lush grass near the base of a huge cottonwood.

Chapter 30

"You taste salty," he said.

"That's sweat, silly."

"Nonsense. Ladies don't sweat. Everybody knows that."
He went back to what he'd been doing, which was sucking
at her right nipple.

"That tickles."

"Excuse me, I won't do it again." He tried to raise up,
but she grabbed the back of his head and pushed him onto
her breast again.

"I said it tickles, I didn't say that I didn't like it."

Her nipple was small and hard and pointy. He opened
wide and sucked flesh into his mouth, and was able to draw
her whole tit in. Lenore moaned and grabbed his hand, pushing it down onto her belly and spreading her thighs apart.

Longarm took the hint and found the spot she wanted
him to find.

She was wet already. His finger slipped inside with ease.
He wiggled it around enough to get it nice and moist, then
withdrew it and began to lightly stroke the warm pink entry
where her clitoris was as erect as her nipple.

Lenore cried out, her body tensing and quivering beneath
his touch. He felt the spasms of pleasure sweep through
her like waves on a seashore, rippling her stomach muscles
and making her pussy clench and contract like a tiny, eager
second mouth.

"I just knew it was a good idea to come to town with
Mama today," she said.

"Sure suits me," he agreed. He shifted over to the other
side and gave the left nipple its due, then kissed the girl.
She sighed.

144

"That was so nice," she said. "Thank you."

"My pleasure, ma'am."

She smiled. "Give me a minute to come down. Then I'll treat you, okay?"

"I'm in no hurry."

"But I am."

"All right then." He rolled onto his back and lay beside her, peering up toward the lacy network of leaves and branches overhead.

"I feel like Eve in the Garden," Lenore said.

"Yeah, but would Eve have been doing this?"

"Of course, dear. That was before there was such a thing as sin." She giggled. "Besides, what else would there have been to do for fun?"

"Reckon it's a subject I haven't given much thought to," he admitted.

"I haven't either. The point is, my fine and handsome stallion, this outdoor air and drifting clouds make me feel free and horny at the same time."

"I ain't complaining."

"Good." She sat up. When he stirred she placed a hand on his chest and pushed him back down again. "Let me play a little now, please."

"Enjoy yourself. Me, I'll just lay here and take a nap." He closed his eyes and turned his head away.

"That, sir, is a challenge."

Longarm grinned but didn't answer.

He felt Lenore shift position at his side. A moment later he could feel her light touch as she gently took him into her hands and ran her fingers up and down his shaft as if examining, and enjoying, the sight and the feel of what he had there.

She cupped his balls in one hand and played with him with the other. She propped herself on top of him, lying across his belly while she continued to fondle his cock.

Another moment more and he was surrounded by wet heat. He smiled. Turnabout wasn't only fair, it was damned nice.

"Hope you can tell how close to ready I am. Otherwise you're apt to get a hot drink like it or not."

145

"I can tell," she murmured. And went right back to what she was doing.

Forewarned was fair play. Longarm kept his eyes closed and gave in to the deep sensations that were building in his groin.

He let himself go limp and loose while Lenore did all the work.

She sucked noisily, greedily on him, and all the while her hands were playing with his balls and stroking the base of his shaft.

Longarm felt the rising tide of pleasure and willed himself to stay relaxed. He didn't tense even when the hot, sweet flow started. He felt the fluids pulse and surge, and Lenore stayed with him, never changing her rhythm as she sucked and pulled on him. He could feel her throat work on top of him and around him, and her hands were gentle on him.

He sighed, and for just a moment had the feeling that he was so light after her draining him that his body had disengaged from his brain and was floating off the bed of crushed grass where they lay.

That sensation, pleasant though it was, couldn't last for long. After a moment Lenore allowed him to slide out of her mouth, and the air felt chill on his wet skin there.

He opened his eyes and looked at her. She was smiling, obviously pleased with herself for what she'd given him. That was all right. He was pleased with her too. She was entitled.

"Nice," he said.

"Thank you." She winked and licked her lips, making a show of running the tip of her tongue over them. Then she laughed and nestled down at his side with one trailing hand cupped warm on him. "You aren't off the hook yet, you know," she said. "Now it's my turn again."

"Oh, I wouldn't forget something as important as all that," he assured her.

"Good." She giggled. "Then, you see, it will be your turn again. Then mine. Then yours. Then—"

"Hey!" he yelped. "What kinda machine d'you think you've got here?"

"Quite a man, actually," Lenore said happily.

"Oh. Well, in *that* case . . ." He smiled. He hugged the girl and held her close, enjoying the feel of her smooth skin and the warm and friendly way she cuddled at his side.

The clouds continued to sail across the sky far above them, and a light breeze sprang up to make the cottonwood branches dance and jiggle, the sunlight coming through the leaves making ever-changing patterns of light and shadow on their twined bodies.

"What a lovely, lovely day," Lenore sighed.

Longarm gave the girl a fond look and decided he couldn't have agreed more.

Chapter 31

Longarm lay drowsing, half asleep and only distantly aware of the pleasant feel of the afternoon breeze wafting warm and nice over bare skin.

Lenore snorted, a most unladylike sound, and he felt her stir at his side. She'd been napping for half an hour or so. If she hadn't awakened soon he would have had to rouse her anyway. He didn't want to keep her there, enjoyable though it damn sure was, so long that her mother became suspicious about what the girl was up to.

"Hi."

"Hi yourself," she said. She was already smiling, and he could guess why. If the pleased and hollow lassitude she felt was anything at all like what he was experiencing, she couldn't help but smile whether she wanted to or not.

"We'd better get dressed now."

She made a pouting face, then quickly smiled again.

Longarm sat up and yawned, stretching. He felt genuinely good after being with this spritely, delightful young woman.

"Once more?" she asked.

"It's getting late," he reminded her.

"Please?"

If she put it that way . . . Hell, it wasn't nice to make a lady beg.

Lenore turned away from him and drew a pile of last fall's leaves to her. She picked through them, ignoring the dried brown ones but collecting a stack of autumn leaves that somehow retained a hint of the bright yellow they once had been.

"I'll pay you," she said, turning back to him and presenting the yellow leaves to him by dropping them onto his lap. "My golden treasure, sir, in exchange for your body." She grinned and reached into the small pile that was in his lap. But ignoring the leaves themselves and burrowing her hand underneath them to something that she found to be of much more interest there.

"If you put it that way, ma'am, why . . . damn!" He stopped, the hand that had been reaching for her freezing in place in midair now.

"Longarm? What is it? Is something wrong?"

"No. No, by damn. Nothing's wrong." He laughed. "You just reminded me of something, that's all."

"Something important?"

"Yeah, something important." He sprang onto his feet and reached down to take her hand and help her upright too. "Get dressed, girl."

"But you said—"

"I know, but I'll have to scratch your itch again later."

"Promise?"

He laughed and kissed her. "Promise."

"I'll hold you to that."

"I hope you do," he assured her. "Go on now. Get yourself dressed."

Longarm pulled his own clothes on quickly, then chafed at the delay while Lenore brushed the leaves and bits of grass off her chunky, sturdy little body and got dressed also.

Even with his help it took her an annoyingly long time to get all those yards and yards of cloth arranged in proper order, all the laces yanked and tied, all the buttons buttoned and hooks hooked.

Dang female fashion anyhow, Longarm thought.

When she was finally presentable again he grabbed up the parasol and shoved it into her hands.

"A girl could almost feel insulted by this rush for the gentleman to get away," she protested.

He gave her a quick, unconvincing kiss and a pat on the backside. "I'll make it up to you later. That's another promise. And I'll explain too if it works out the way I think it will."

That seemed to satisfy her. She smiled at him and led the way out of the willows to the town street that was only a matter of paces away from the hidden trysting spot she had found for them.

Chapter 32

Longarm found Carl Worley busy testifying at a Magistrate's Court session on the second floor of the City Hall building. The lineup of cases on the docket for the day was the usual assortment of public drunkenness, horse racing on town streets, excessive noise, and public nuisance. Longarm slipped inside the tiny courtroom and stood at the back waiting to catch Worley's eye while the magistrate mechanically levied two-and three-dollar fines.

"Pardon me, your honor. Could we have a five-minute recess while I confer with a colleague?" the police chief asked when he spotted Longarm.

The magistrate frowned, but granted the request with a loud slap of his gavel. Longarm didn't think he'd ever seen a small-time judge who wasn't fond of the sound of his own gavel, and this one was no exception.

"What is it, Longarm? You look rarin' to go."

"I am," Longarm admitted with a grin. "I'm gonna go out and wait for our killers to show up."

Worley's eyebrows shot up.

"What I wanted t' know, Carl, was if you figure to come with me. Not that it's strictly necessary. Just thought you might like to."

"Damn right I'd like to. Tyrone Day's murder and all those others didn't happen in my bailiwick, but Tom Jepp's sure as hell did. I'd like to be there at the finish of it."

"Good." Longarm smiled. " 'Cause I'm gonna need the borrow of that horse of yours again."

Worley turned and from the back of the small courtroom said, "Larry, I have to leave now." He neglected the normally obligatory "your honor" this time, Longarm noticed.

The magistrate looked up from the papers he'd been reading. "Dammit, Chief, you can't leave now. We're in session here, you know."

"Got to, Larry. I'll explain later."

"But what am I supposed to do with all these cases, Chief?"

"Hell, Larry, I don't know. Turn them loose if you can't get along without me today."

"You get yourself back here, Chief, or I just might hold you in contempt."

"Later, Larry. We'll talk about this later." Worley motioned for Longarm to join him as he turned his back on the magistrate and walked out of the courtroom.

The Santa Fe Rail Road, which did not and never would reach Santa Fe, had a southbound freight for Lamy that was running behind schedule.

The conductor bitched and moaned about this further delay, but was amenable to subtle suggestion. The suggestion, Longarm's, was that he either transport two peace officers and two horses or face a federal charge of interference with an officer.

"If you put it that way . . ."

"I do," Longarm assured him.

"Every car on the damn train is full. I can carry you, but I don't have room for those horses."

"Add a car," Longarm insisted.

"Do you know how long that would take?"

"Longer than your jail term, d'you think?" Longarm asked.

"I'll add a boxcar," the conductor said. Moaning and groaning, he stalked off to give the orders. At the same time the telegraph operator had to have new running orders issued.

This change was going to fuck up the scheduling of every train on the Santa Fe rails today, Longarm knew. He figured that was a small price to pay for the capture of two murderers—all that remained alive and moving at this point in the string of conspirators that had started back in Colorado—but he didn't necessarily expect the Santa Fe conductor to agree with him. Which was probably just as well.

"Do you know what you're doing?" Worley whispered after the railroad conductor was on his way.

"If I don't, Carl, I might come back and apply for a job as one of your police officers."

"You'd look all right in the coat, but I can't quite visualize you wearing one of those caps," Worley said with a chuckle.

"Thanks for coming with me, Carl. I figure if the jurisdiction is shaky anyhow, and it damn sure is, I might as well confuse it all the more by having you along. Besides, to tell you the truth, I'm not sure just who I might be able to trust south of here. It's beginning to look like half the people in this country . . . well, never mind about that. Let's just say that I trust you."

"Whatever you say, Longarm. I know Tom Jepp went bad for some reason, but when I knew the man I liked and respected him. I'd like to see his killing and those others cleared off the books."

"That's good enough for me, Carl."

The two men waited patiently while the Santa Fe engineer moved his clanking freight onto a siding and picked up a boxcar. Instead of remaking the whole train they hooked it on behind the caboose, and carried a plank ramp to it so they could load Carl Worley's saddle horses into the car.

"There's a short siding and loading chutes near the old Pigeon Ranch," the conductor said. "I'll take you there, but I won't hang around and unload you. I'll drop the damn car and leave it there for you. You and the chief here can ride in the car with the horses. When we get there it'll just be a stop and go, Deputy. The brakeman will turn the screws on this car and snap the connection, then we're off. From there you're on your own."

"That's fair enough," Longarm agreed. He thought the train conductor looked relieved to hear it.

"Come on, Carl." Longarm and the Las Vegas police chief climbed into the nearly empty boxcar with Worley's horses. The conductor checked to see that everything in the car was secure, then slid the boxcar door closed. Moments later the late-running freight pulled forward.

Chapter 33

"That son of a bitch." Longarm was more amused than pissed when he said it.

"He got you," Worley agreed.

"So he did." Longarm chuckled and tugged once more on the boxcar door, but the thing wouldn't budge. The latch had been set when the door was closed, and no one inside the car could reach it to pull it open. They could still hear the Santa Fe freight pulling south away from the siding where the extra car had been dropped.

Still, it was only an annoyance, a way for the conductor to tweak Longarm's nose without doing any real harm. And if he was questioned about it later he could claim it was a mere oversight and certainly not intentional, no, sir. He'd simply forgotten that detail in his rush to get the train back on schedule after doing just exactly what the federal deputy asked, sir.

Still chuckling, Longarm climbed the steel rungs bolted onto the back wall of the boxcar interior and wrestled open the trapdoor on the roof. The trapdoor was useful for coming and going from the car while a train was in motion, and useful also to load grain from an elevator. But it damn sure wasn't used very often for any purpose. By the time Longarm had the heavy thing open and shoved out of the way, he had grit and wood splinters down the back of his collar and grime all over himself. The conductor had gotten his revenge rather nicely, Longarm acknowledged.

While Worley held the horses, Longarm climbed down the outside of the car to the ground and walked around to the door so he could free the latch and haul the big sliding door open.

"The SOB didn't line us up at the loading chute either, Carl. We'll have to jump them horses down."

Worley didn't find that so funny, but there wasn't much choice about it. He forced first one horse out and then the other. At least the roadbed was fairly level there and the horses did not have to jump out of the boxcar onto a steep gravel slope. They made it to the ground with injuries no more serious than a skinned knee on the bay Longarm was riding again today.

"We'll give them a minute to settle," Longarm said. He pulled out a pair of cheroots and offered one to Worley, then lit both.

"You wouldn't happen to know where we're going, would you?" the Las Vegas police chief asked.

"As a matter o' fact, Carl . . . no." Longarm grinned.

After the nuisance of having to unload his horses from a freight car without benefit of a ramp, Worley did not look amused.

"I'm not trying to keep you in the dark, Carl. I honestly don't know," Longarm admitted.

"But—"

"Somewhere down here. I'm sure of that."

"I don't understand, dammit."

"It's all guesswork, okay? But it's the only thing I can think of that fits. Those boys were all part of General Sibley's invasion that was supposed to capture Colorado for the Confederacy, right?"

"What could that have to do with these murders now? That's what I don't understand, Longarm."

"That's what I didn't understand either until I remembered something Moses Barnett told me the first time I talked to him. Sibley, with Frazier and Jepp and all them boys in his column, was doing just fine until they got into Glorietta Pass back there." The Santa Fe train had labored its way up and over the low pass not half an hour earlier.

"That's where Chivington's Coloradans met them and whipped them and drove them clear back to Texas as a bunch of straggling, beaten small units," Longarm explained.

"All right."

155

"The thing that I knew and didn't pay attention to was that until they got to Glorietta, those boys had been having themselves a helluva good time. They beat Canby outside Santa Fe and then virtually sacked the city."

"Yes?"

"Carl, that bunch of Texas irregulars raped and stole and had themselves a hell of a time. *So what happened to all the loot they carried with them when they marched out of Santa Fe?*"

"Shit," Worley exclaimed.

"Deep shit," Longarm agreed. "Gold coin, Carl. Gold trappings from all those fine old churches, prob'ly. Who knows what else. There must've been a mountain of the stuff. Gold and silver too. And Frazier's company was guarding the pack train that day."

"Ty Day paid for that wagon with Spanish-minted gold coins," Worley observed.

"Exactly. And don't it stand to reason that there would have been some Spanish coins still circulating in Santa Fe then when it was only a generation since the town was part of a Spanish colony? Only twenty years or so since it was Mexican?"

"Hell, yes."

"I never heard anything about Sibley's loot being recovered and returned to the people of Santa Fe, Carl."

"It isn't something I've ever paid attention to, particularly, but I guess I never heard anything about that either," Worley said. "You think . . . ?"

"I think Frazier and some of his men saved that pack string of booty from Chivington an' decided to keep it for themselves. The invasion force was breaking apart, after all. Chivington had them in a rout. They could see that for themselves. I'm guessing they hid it somewhere, and the ones in the know agreed to go into hiding and divvy the loot up among them sometime later. Then something happened. Prob'ly they didn't all know where it was. But someone had to. Maybe the work detail that actually hid the loot was ambushed later and most of them killed. That crazy old man in Trinidad had been scalped once. It could even have happened when he was on his way back to Texas from

156

here. If that was so, it would explain a lot. Like all the others not knowing where to find the cache.

"And I'm guessing that it was K. C. Caswell who knew where to find the key to the whole thing. Caswell got into a fight up in Colorado and landed himself in the territorial prison where he couldn't get out to the gold and nobody else could get in to him. Even if they could go in and talk to him—as visitors, say—the man wasn't going to give the secret away and trust the others to keep his share for him. I'm thinking that's why nobody started to move on this until Caswell served out his time and was released from the state prison. That's when hell started to pop over this.

"Caswell went straight to Trinidad and murdered that old halfwit who may or may not have been a Confederate officer too. And stole a Paterson Colt from him, though Lord knows what the hell that could have to do with it. That gun keeps turning up missing even though we keep finding bodies right along.

"I'm thinking that this old man in Trinidad had whatever Caswell needed to recover the loot. I'd think it was that gun, except that I can't see how an antique pistol would mean anything. Anyhow, whatever the key was, a map or whatever, Caswell got it from the old man in Trinidad. Then Jepp murdered Caswell to get it off him and so on right down the line. The old wartime buddies aren't buddies anymore, Carl. And they're all wanting all the loot for themselves now that it's come time to make the split. It must be a hell of an amount to cause this trail of blood and to make men as respectable as a Texas Ranger and a Colorado judge chuck everything and walk away from the lives they'd made for themselves since the war."

"It was a big wagon Tyrone Day thought he'd need for the job," Worley said.

"Day's mistake was thinking he could trust the Budde brothers to help him with the job. Instead they killed him."

"Unless," Worley suggested, "it was the Buddes who killed Tom Jepp to begin with. And Day knew they'd done it and came out with that wagon demanding to go along and collect his share."

"Possible. We'll ask Bud and Tony when they get here.

Jason Budde and Anthony Brice, I suppose I should say, since that's who they really are."

"Here?"

"They have to come this way. If I'm right with my guessing," Longarm said, "those boys are headed this way. They'll come through Glorietta Pass and head toward Apache Canyon, wherever that is. That's where the unit was last in action and where that pack train was last known to be. They had a head start on us from Las Vegas, but the train should have put us ahead of them now. Now what we need to do is wait for them along the road and nail them when they show up."

"I've ridden this road before, Longarm. The old road doesn't follow the rails exactly, but it isn't far. Right up there a quarter mile or so. Apache Canyon is over that way." Worley pointed.

"So if we pick a spot along the road between Glorietta and Apache, we should intercept them pretty as you please."

"Let's get to it."

Chapter 34

Carl Worley shook his head. "That isn't them, Longarm."

That was another reason why Longarm had wanted Worley along. He knew the Budde brothers by sight. Longarm didn't. And having Worley there to identify the men seemed a helluva lot better idea than setting up a roadblock and trying to interrogate everyone who passed along this road.

Longarm sat back down and watched the springboard wagon carrying two men rumble along the road below with no idea that they were being observed by two lawmen hiding in ambush.

The wait was taking longer than Longarm expected. He was beginning to wonder if he'd figured this thing wrong and if the Buddes—one real Budde and a pal named Brice, really—weren't coming after all.

Longarm was accustomed to waiting, but there was one thing that annoyed him every time he had to do it. He couldn't smoke while he was lying in ambush like this, dammit. A stray puff of white smoke would give a person away as quick as a white flag.

Instead Longarm made do with a sip of water from one of the canteens Worley had provided. The horses now were hidden a quarter mile away in a small canyon where they would be out of sight and, equally as important, out of smelling distance from the public road. Longarm didn't want any whinnying sonuvabitch of a saddle horse giving the deal away.

Carl Worley too seemed used to this sort of waiting. Worley sat with his back propped against a slab of red rock and a Winchester rifle laid over his knees. Longarm's Winchester was back in his rented room in Denver. Because, after all, he'd only been taking a train down to Trinidad and straight back home to Denver when he left, hadn't he? He should have known better.

A horseman crested the rise to the east of their ambush site and rode toward Apache Canyon at a slow lope. Longarm looked at Carl Worley. It wasn't impossible that Jason Budde or Anthony Brice could be riding alone by now. So far there were plenty of old wartime friends who seemed perfectly willing to slaughter each other for General Sibley's Santa Fe loot.

"Nope," Worley said. "I never saw this man before."

Longarm cleared his throat and spat. He sure did wish he could have a smoke.

The horseman jogged past beneath their hiding place and continued on to the west. From here the roads curled west and then slightly north again to reach Santa Fe, or dropped south along the Rio Grande Valley toward the Tularosa basin and distant Las Cruces. There was more traffic along this road than Longarm would have expected now that the railroad should be satisfying most of the freight and passenger requirements here.

"What do you want to do if it gets dark before they come?" Worley asked.

"Move down closer to the road, I suppose, and keep on watching. For sure I'm not letting them past without a scuffle," Longarm said. "We have no idea which way they'll be going once they reach Apache Canyon."

"Never mind," Worley said. "We don't have to worry about it now." He pointed toward the east. There was another wagon rolling into view.

"That's them?"

"I'm pretty sure it is. Let 'em get a little closer and I'll tell you for sure."

The wagon, with two men seated on the tall box, was a heavy-duty freight rig drawn by six thick-bodied cobs. Even at a distance the banging and clattering of the box riding atop the running gear said that the wagon was empty at the moment.

If this was Budde and Brice, Longarm saw, it was no wonder they were so long in getting here. The six-up pulling the wagon was powerful but slow. The men must have ridden their saddle horses part of the way and then bought or stolen this freight rig so they could pile it full of gold and silver loot from a war they hadn't forgotten. That *vaquero* back at their ranch had said they'd left there on saddle horses, though. They hadn't started out with a wagon.

"That's them," Worley confirmed as they drew within a hundred yards and continued to roll into the ambush. "I'm sure of it now."

"All right, Carl. We'll take them the easy way if we can, just like we talked about. Cover me."

"You got it."

Longarm left the slab of flat rock he'd been sitting on for several hours and slid down a steep, gravel bank to reach the roadside.

The waiting point had been chosen with care. Longarm was hidden behind the boulders of an old rock spill as he dropped down to the road level. Budde and Brice couldn't see him, nor could Longarm look eastward along the road now, but Worley and his rifle commanded a broad field of fire if it should come to that.

Longarm stood out of sight beside the road and looked up. He couldn't see Carl from down here. The police chief was too far back from the edge of the cutbank. That was all right. The idea was for Budde and Brice to not be able to see him either.

Once they were under two guns widely separated high and low they would have no choice but to give themselves up. A fight would be suicidal once they saw what they were facing, and a nice, meek surrender was exactly what Longarm wanted. In his judgment handcuffs were always more pleasant than handguns when it came to making an arrest.

The wagon was close now. Longarm could hear the light, chiming tinkle of trace chains and the deeper, rolling crunch of iron-tired wheels rumbling across gravel. He palmed his Colt in one hand and his opened wallet to display his badge in the other. This one could go nice and easy and right by the book.

He could hear the thud of hoofs the size of dinner plates

smacking the hard ground and the clatter of the empty wagon box bouncing on the frame.

A few yards more and Longarm could step out and stop them and it would all be over. He held the Colt Thunderer chest high and cleared his throat.

Ready . . .

A rifle shot crashed overhead, and a horse snorted in terror.

"Hey . . . !"

Longarm heard Carl Worley's rifle action work, and then there was the dull, reverberating boom of another gunshot.

Longarm threw himself forward in a rolling dive, Colt held ready as he sprawled into the middle of the road, rolled onto his belly, and searched frantically for a target.

There wasn't any target in sight, but there was something a damn sight worse.

The six-up of heavy, rearing horses came down onto all fours and bolted forward in a panic.

Six horses and a freight wagon tore forward along the road.

And Longarm was lying square in the middle of that road.

Chapter 35

Longarm shouted.

That wasn't going to do *any* damn good.

The big horses had broken into a terrified gallop and were charging blindly forward. There was no sign of the Buddes on the driving box now, and the reins flopped loose on the ground as the panicked six-up thundered straight toward Longarm.

Two dozen murderous hoofs driving probably four tons of crushing weight careened down on him.

Up on top of the cutbank Carl Worley's Winchester banged again, but if he hit any of the horses it wasn't enough to stop the runaway now.

Longarm gathered his knees under him and flung himself sideways.

He triggered a pistol shot in the general direction of the wagon in the scant hope that he might knock one of the leaders down.

His shot didn't do any more good than Carl's had, and now all he could see looming high above him were white eyeballs and distended nostrils and slobbering muzzles as the fear-driven horses charged down on him.

Longarm managed to get partially out of the way. He was in midair, trying to jump to safety, when the off leader hit him.

Longarm felt the impact of its foreleg on his thigh.

He felt himself lifted, spinning through the air like a damned boomerang.

He hit the ground and slid, rolling and tumbling now.

The freight wagon rumbled past, its right side wheels missing his legs by less than a yard.

A yard was fine. A yard was wonderful. One lousy inch would have been enough. Just so those iron tires didn't chop through him like scythes.

He struggled to his feet, still hanging on to the Thunderer, and shakily aimed down the road toward the back of the moving wagon.

Budde and Brice were out of sight inside the box, though, and the runaway team was still charging forward in a mad gallop. From ground level the horses were protected by the wagon box, and Longarm couldn't get a shot at them.

Carl Worley with his longer-ranging Winchester ran over to the edge of the cutbank, took careful aim, and fired.

Ninety or a hundred yards down the road one of the big horses snorted and tossed its head. The animal staggered, its suddenly slowed speed skewing the pull on the doubletree and making the wagon go into a slide.

The horse Worley'd shot fell, and the wheeler behind it fought the traces and ran halfway up its back before all of them came to a halt. The wagon they'd been pulling broke free of the linchpin and crashed off the road, where it overturned with the sound of splintering wood and uselessly spinning wheels.

"Jesus, Carl, what happened?"

"It's my fault, Longarm," Worley groaned. "I stood up to take aim, just in case, and Bud saw me. He went for his gun, and I had to shoot him. I should've waited for you to start it before I moved. But I didn't and then Bud spotted me . . . it was just lousy luck that he was looking up this way when I tried to get into position . . . and then . . . are you all right?"

"Yeah. Yeah, I'm all right."

Worley slid down the embankment to the road level.

Longarm tried an experimental step in the direction of the overturned wagon. His leg hurt like hell but seemed to be working all right. The horse had kicked him, but the leg hadn't been planted on the ground at the time. There'd been no resistance to the impact, and nothing was broken now. A good bruise and a few days of minor pain would be the worst he could expect. Thank goodness.

"You said you shot Budde. What about Brice?"

"Don't know. I snapped one at him, but I don't know if I hit him or not," Worley said.

"Then let's go real easy."

Longarm and Worley advanced slowly toward the wrecked wagon. They stayed on opposite sides of the road and held their weapons at the ready, just in case Brice popped up with a gun in his hand.

Longarm was pleased to discover that his leg was giving him less pain as he moved further, the exercise of walking helping to warm and limber his battered muscles. He was limping a little, but was able to move all right.

"If you like, Longarm, you can sit here. I'll tidy things up at the wagon and come back for you."

"I'm all right, Carl."

"You're limping."

"It's okay. Really."

"Whatever you say."

They came within twenty yards of the wagon. Then ten. There was no sign of Brice or Budde, either one. The five remaining horses, sweat-lathered more from their panic than from the exertions of that short run, stood head down in their traces, as far from the dead horse as they could manage inside the close confinement of the harness.

"Slow and easy now, Carl," Longarm advised. They inched ahead, Longarm circling out to the right and Worley to the left.

After a moment Longarm sighed and pushed the Thunderer back into his holster. "You can relax, Carl. Neither of those fellas is going anywhere now."

"You're sure? I can't see anything over here."

"I can see 'em. They're both on the ground on this side."

The two bodies were sprawled in the roadside brush like a pair of rag dolls. No live human could twist into the pretzel shapes these had taken on. If Worley hadn't killed both of them, then the wagon wreck sure had.

Longarm checked the nearer of the bodies. It was Jason Budde. He had a bullet hole square over his heart and hadn't lived to feel the wreck.

Longarm stepped over Budde's body. Worley, he saw, was taking care of the team, removing the traces from the horse he'd shot and maneuvering the others clear.

"Well I'll be damned," Longarm muttered when he stood over Anthony Brice's broken body. Brice hadn't lived long enough to feel the wreck either. Carl Worley's snap shot had drilled a hole in the center of Brice's forehead.

Longarm knelt, the leg giving him some pain when he bent it, and checked the contents of Brice's pockets.

As the older and formerly senior of the two Mounted Volunteers, Brice was the more likely of them to be carrying the key to the Santa Fe treasure.

There was nothing in his pockets, though, except money, a folding knife, and a much-used handkerchief.

The handkerchief—Longarm looked—had nothing on it but dried snot. There wasn't any map drawn on it.

Longarm went back to Budde's body and inspected it. Jason Budde had been carrying less on him than Brice when they died.

Closer to the road Worley was busy now trying to push the wagon, or what was left of it, back onto its wheels.

"That isn't going to do any good, Carl. Do you see any luggage around here?"

"No, nothing."

Longarm grunted. Surely Budde and Brice hadn't committed the treasure-finding directions to memory and destroyed the map to it. It'd be quite a kick in the teeth to everybody if that had happened, Longarm realized. All this dying. All of it to no purpose.

Worley had given up trying to right the shattered wagon and was kicking around in the brush now. He bent over and came up with a set of saddlebags. Longarm could see a saddle lying half hidden on the ground there too. The contents of the wagon had been strewn in all directions when the rig crashed, apparently.

"What'd you find, Carl?"

"Let me look." Worley opened the saddlebags, glanced inside, and shrugged. "Laundry."

"Damn."

"Yeah." Worley draped the saddlebags over his shoulder. "Why don't you keep looking, Longarm. I'll go get the horses and bring them here. No point in you walking on that leg any more'n you have to."

"That's real considerate of you, Carl."

"I don't mind." Worley started off in the direction of the canyon where the horses had been hidden.

"Carl."

"Yes, Longarm?"

"Why don't you leave the saddlebags here, huh?"

"Ah, it's no trouble to carry them. They aren't heavy. And I'll be wanting to return those boys' personal effects for them. That's the least I can do for 'em." He smiled.

"Carl," Longarm repeated. "I'd really like you to leave those bags here."

"But it's no bother. Really." He smiled again. "Stay right there, Longarm. I'll be back with the horses in no time." He turned away.

"Carl!"

There was a sharp, cutting edge to Longarm's tone of voice this time.

Worley stopped.

"I'm gonna look inside those saddlebags, Carl. I'd rather you didn't try and keep me from it."

Worley's shoulders sagged. "You, uh, have it figured, don't you?"

"Yeah, I expect I do, Carl. Neither of those boys saw you. You waited for them and you shot them down from ambush. You weren't going to take any chance on them surrendering peaceful-like, were you." It wasn't really a question. "Nobody places bullets that perfect with a hurry-up snap shot, Carl. What you did back there was murder. And now you've found what you murdered them for. Is it worth it, Carl?"

Worley looked like he was going to deny it. Then he looked more closely at Longarm's eyes and decided not to bother trying.

"It was worth it," the Las Vegas police chief said. "If you'd ever seen what was loaded onto that pack string . . ."

"Were you part of it too, Carl?"

"Not the Mounted Volunteers, no. I was with the Sibley expedition, but I wasn't any fancy dragoon. I was with a company of irregular infantry. I was there at Santa Fe. My squad helped load the mules that the dragoons were guarding. So I saw all that gold, but I never got to touch any of it. Never knew what happened to it afterward."

"Until lately?" Longarm asked.

"Until lately," Worley agreed.

"Did you have it figured before me?"

"Sure. But not until after Jepp's murder. I didn't kill Tom, I surely didn't. Wouldn't have known to, you see. Not until you got to talking to me and comparing notes and getting that information about people who all used to be with Sibley. That's when I knew what was happening." Worley laughed bitterly. "You want to hear something funny? I thought it was Day that killed Tom. That's what I went to see him about the morning he died. I knew from talking with him over the years that Ty had been with the dragoons. I talked to him that morning and tried to get in on the action, but Day hadn't known anything about Jepp being in town. Jepp and Brice . . . I guess they'd been close back in the old days and Tom was trying to be square with Tony and make it a fair split . . . they weren't going to let Day in on it. It was likely Bud who killed Tom. And I suppose he would've killed Tony too sooner or later or been killed by him. Anyhow, Day found out from me that Jepp had been killed. Day knew Bud and Tony from the war and figured out what was going on. That's why he went out to the Budde place and got himself shot."

"And the map?" Longarm asked.

"Day knew about the map. He was supposed to've been a part of it all. I didn't know there was such a thing. From what he told me, Longarm, your guesswork was pretty accurate." He smiled. "For whatever that's worth."

"And the Paterson gun?"

"The map is supposed to be inscribed on the inside of the grips. Scrimshaw, Day called it. Whatever that is."

"And the gun, I take it, is in the saddlebags you're carrying?"

Worley's flicker of smile was enough of an answer. "I tried, Longarm. You got to admit that I tried. I tried to slip away from here without killing you."

"Bullshit," Longarm snorted. "You could've dropped that horse easy when you thought I was gonna be run over. You didn't, though. You just fired wild to keep those horses scared and running. You were hoping the wagon team would kill me and save you the trouble."

"But just now I tried to walk away and leave you here. Now you got to admit to that, Longarm."

"What I got to admit, Carl, is that you're scared to face me with a gun. And that, Carl, is the best judgment you've shown all day long."

"We could split the treasure, Longarm. There's more than enough for two."

"No sale, Carl. That loot belongs to whoever it was taken from."

"It's the spoils of war, Longarm. And that war is a long time over. Nobody could figure out now who the original owners were."

"That's for lawyers and courts and claimants to work out."

"I don't want to kill you, Longarm. I really don't."

"Bullshit," Longarm repeated. "The truth is that you can't. And we both know it. You can try me and be buried for your trouble, Carl, or you can surrender those saddlebags and yourself and take your chances in a court-room."

"You'd charge me for killing those two murdering ex-dragoons?"

"If you're alive to answer the charges, I certainly will."

Worley chewed on his lower lip. He seemed nervous now. Longarm could see sweat beading the police chief's forehead. And it wasn't all that hot a day.

Carl Worley trembled and looked for a moment like he was going to break into tears.

It wasn't tears that finally broke, though. It was his nerve.

He dropped the saddlebags onto the ground, shucked his gunbelt, and turned with his wrists extended meekly behind him for Longarm to apply the irons.

Longarm couldn't help wondering, as he limped forward and pulled out his handcuffs, whether any of the greedy former Confederates would think their Santa Fe treasure was worth all this now. If, that is, they'd been alive to answer that question.

It didn't seem real likely, he decided as he snapped the bracelets tight around Carl Worley's wrists.

Not real likely at all.

Watch for

LONGARM AND THE RIVER OF DEATH

152d in the bold LONGARM series from Jove

Coming in August!

GILES TIPPETTE

Author of the best-selling WILSON YOUNG SERIES,
BAD NEWS, and CROSS FIRE is back with his most
exciting Western adventure yet!

JAILBREAK

Time is running out for Justa Williams, owner of the Half-
Moon Ranch in West Texas. His brother Norris is being
held in a Mexican jail, and neither bribes nor threats can
free him.

Now, with the help of a dozen kill-crazy Mex-
ican *banditos*, Justa aims to blast Norris out. But the worst
is yet to come: a hundred-mile chase across the Mexican
desert with fifty *federales* in hot pursuit.

The odds of reaching the Texas border are a million to nothing . . . and if the Williams brothers don't watch their backs,
the road to freedom could turn into the road to hell!

Turn the page for an exciting chapter from

JAILBREAK
by
Giles Tippette

On sale now, wherever Jove Books are sold!

At supper Norris, my middle brother, said, "I think we got some trouble on that five thousand acres down on the border near Laredo."

He said it serious, which is the way Norris generally says everything. I quit wrestling with the steak Buttercup, our cook, had turned into rawhide and said, "What are you talking about? How could we have trouble on land lying idle?"

He said, "I got word from town this afternoon that a telegram had come in from a friend of ours down there. He says we got some kind of squatters taking up residence on the place."

My youngest brother, Ben, put his fork down and said, incredulously, "*That* five thousand acres? Hell, it ain't nothing but rocks and cactus and sand. Why in hell would anyone want to squat on that worthless piece of nothing?"

Norris just shook his head. "I don't know. But that's what the telegram said. Came from Jack Cole. And if anyone ought to know what's going on down there it would be him."

I thought about it and it didn't make a bit of sense. I was Justa Williams, and my family, my two brothers and myself and our father, Howard, occupied a considerable ranch called the Half-Moon down along the Gulf of Mexico in Matagorda County, Texas. It was some of the best grazing land in the state and we had one of the best herds of purebred and crossbred cattle in that part of the country. In short we were pretty well-to-do.

But that didn't make us any the less ready to be stolen from, if indeed that was the case. The five thousand acres Norris had been talking about had come to us through a trade

175

our father had made some years before. We'd never made any use of the land, mainly because, as Ben had said, it was pretty worthless and because it was a good two hundred miles from our ranch headquarters. On a few occasions we'd bought cattle in Mexico and then used the acreage to hold small groups on while we made up a herd. But other than that, it lay mainly forgotten.

I frowned. "Norris, this doesn't make a damn bit of sense. Right after supper send a man into Blessing with a return wire for Jack asking him if he's certain. What the hell kind of squatting could anybody be doing on that land?"

Ben said, "Maybe they're raisin' watermelons." He laughed.

I said, "They could raise melons, but there damn sure wouldn't be no water in them."

Norris said, "Well, it bears looking into." He got up, throwing his napkin on the table. "I'll go write out that telegram."

I watched him go, dressed, as always, in his town clothes. Norris was the businessman in the family. He'd been sent down to the University at Austin and had got considerable learning about the ins and outs of banking and land deals and all the other parts of our business that didn't directly involve the ranch. At the age of twenty-nine I'd been the boss of the operation a good deal longer than I cared to think about. It had been thrust upon me by our father when I wasn't much more than twenty. He'd said he'd wanted me to take over while he was still strong enough to help me out of my mistakes and I reckoned that was partly true. But it had just seemed that after our mother had died the life had sort of gone out of him. He'd been one of the earliest settlers, taking up the land not long after Texas had become a republic in 1845. I figured all the years of fighting Indians and then Yankees and scalawags and carpetbaggers and cattle thieves had taken their toll on him. Then a few years back he'd been nicked in the lungs by a bullet that should never have been allowed to heed his way and it had thrown an extra strain on his heart. He was pushing seventy and he still had plenty of head on his shoulders, but mostly all he did now was sit around in his rocking chair and stare out over the cattle and land business he'd built. Not to say that I didn't go to him for advice when the occasion demanded. I did, and mostly I took it.

Buttercup came in just then and sat down at the end of the table with a cup of coffee. He was near as old as Dad and almost completely worthless. But he'd been one of the first hands that Dad had hired and he'd been kept on even after he couldn't sit a horse anymore. The problem was he'd elected himself cook, and that was the sorriest day our family had ever seen. There were two Mexican women hired to cook for the twelve riders we kept full time, but Buttercup insisted on cooking for the family.

Mainly, I think, because he thought he was one of the family. A notion we could never completely dissuade him from.

So he sat there, about two days of stubble on his face, looking as scrawny as a pecked-out rooster, sweat running down his face, his apron a mess. He said, wiping his forearm across his forehead, "Boy, it shore be hot in there. You boys shore better be glad you ain't got no business takes you in that kitchen."

Ben said, in a loud mutter, "I wish you didn't either."

Ben, at twenty-five, was easily the best man with a horse or a gun that I had ever seen. His only drawback was that he was hotheaded and he tended to act first and think later. That ain't a real good combination for someone that could go on the prod as fast as Ben. When I had argued with Dad about taking over as boss, suggesting instead that Norris, with his education, was a much better choice, Dad had simply said, "Yes, in some ways. But he can't handle Ben. You can. You can handle Norris, too. But none of them can handle you."

Well, that hadn't been exactly true. If Dad had wished it I would have taken orders from Norris even though he was two years younger than me. But the logic in Dad's line of thinking had been that the Half-Moon and our cattle business was the lodestone of all our businesses and only I could run that. He had been right. In the past I'd imported purebred Whiteface and Hereford cattle from up North, bred them to our native Longhorns and produced cattle that would bring twice as much at market as the horse-killing, all-bone, all-wild Longhorns. My neighbors had laughed at me at first, claiming those square little purebreds would never make it in our Texas heat. But they'd been wrong and, one by one, they'd followed the example of the Half-Moon.

Buttercup was setting up to take off on another one of his long-winded harangues about how it had been in the "old days" so I quickly got up, excusing myself, and went into the big office we used for sitting around in as well as a place of business. Norris was at the desk composing his telegram so I poured myself out a whiskey and sat down. I didn't want to hear about any trouble over some worthless five thousand acres of borderland. In fact I didn't want to hear about any troubles of any kind. I was just two weeks short of getting married, married to a lady I'd been courting off and on for five years, and I was mighty anxious that nothing come up to interfere with our plans. Her name was Nora Parker and her daddy owned and run the general mercantile in our nearest town, Blessing. I'd almost lost her once before to a Kansas City drummer. She'd finally gotten tired of waiting on me, waiting until the ranch didn't occupy all my time, and almost run off with a smooth-talking Kansas City drummer that called on her daddy in the harness trade. But she'd come to her senses in time and got off the train in Texarkana and returned home.

But even then it had been a close thing. I, along with my men and brothers and help from some of our neighbors, had been involved with stopping a huge herd of illegal cattle being driven up from Mexico from crossing our range and infecting our cattle with tick fever, which could have wiped us all out. I tell you it had been a bloody business. We'd lost four good men and had to kill at least a half dozen on the other side. Fact of the business was I'd come about as close as I ever had to getting killed myself, and that was going some for the sort of rough-and-tumble life I'd led.

Nora had almost quit me over it; saying she just couldn't take the uncertainty. But in the end, she'd stuck by me. That had been the year before, 1896, and I'd convinced her that civilized law was coming to the country, but until it did,

178

we that had been there before might have to take things into our own hands from time to time.

She'd seen that and had understood. I loved her and she loved me and that was enough to overcome any of the trouble we were still likely to encounter from day to day.

So I was giving Norris a pretty sour look as he finished his telegram and sent for a hired hand to ride it into Blessing, seven miles away. I said, "Norris, let's don't make a big fuss about this. That land ain't even crossed my mind in at least a couple of years. Likely we got a few Mexican families squatting down there and trying to scratch out a few acres of corn."

Norris gave me his businessman's look. He said, "It's our land, Justa. And if we allow anyone to squat on it for long enough or put up a fence they can lay claim. That's the law. My job is to see that we protect what we have, not give it away."

I sipped at my whiskey and studied Norris. In his town clothes he didn't look very impressive. He'd inherited more from our mother than from Dad so he was not as wide-shouldered and slim-hipped as Ben and me. But I knew him to be a good, strong, dependable man in any kind of fight. Of course he wasn't that good with a gun, but then Ben and I weren't all that good with books like he was. But I said, just to jolly him a bit, "Norris, I do believe you are running to suet. I may have to put you out with Ben working the horse herd and work a little of that fat off you."

Naturally it got his goat. Norris had always envied Ben and me a little. I was just over six foot and weighed right around a hundred and ninety. I had inherited my daddy's big hands and big shoulders. Ben was almost a copy of me except he was about a size smaller. Norris said, "I weigh the same as I have for the last five years. If it's any of your business."

I said, as if I was being serious, "Must be them sack suits you wear. What they do, pad them around the middle?"

He said, "Why don't you just go to hell."

After he'd stomped out of the room I got the bottle of whiskey and an extra glass and went down to Dad's room. It had been one of his bad days and he'd taken to bed right after lunch. Strictly speaking he wasn't supposed to have no whiskey, but I watered him down a shot every now and then and it didn't seem to do him no harm.

He was sitting up when I came in the room. I took a moment to fix him a little drink, using some water out of his pitcher, then handed him the glass and sat down in the easy chair by the bed. I told him what Norris had reported and asked what he thought.

He took a sip of his drink and shook his head. "Beats all I ever heard," he said. "I took that land in trade for a bad debt some fifteen, twenty years ago. I reckon I'd of been money ahead if I'd of hung on to the bad debt. That land won't even raise weeds, well as I remember, and Noah was in on the last rain that fell on the place."

We had considerable amounts of land spotted around the state as a result of this kind of trade or that. It was Norris's business to keep up with their management. I was just bringing this to Dad's attention more out of boredom and impatience for my wedding day to arrive than anything else.

I said, "Well, it's a mystery to me. How you feeling?"

He half smiled. "Old." Then he looked into his glass. "And I never liked watered whiskey. Pour me a dollop of the straight stuff in here."

I said, "Now, Howard. You know—"

He cut me off. "If I wanted somebody to argue with I'd send for Buttercup. Now do like I told you."

I did, but I felt guilty about it. He took the slug of whiskey down in one pull. Then he leaned his head back on the pillow and said, "Aaaaah. I don't give a damn what that horse doctor says, ain't nothing makes a man feel as good inside as a shot of the best."

I felt sorry for him lying there. He'd always led just the kind of life he wanted—going where he wanted, doing what he wanted, having what he set out to get. And now he was reduced to being a semi-invalid. But one thing that showed the strength that was still in him was that you *never* heard him complain. He said, "How's the cattle?"

I said, "They're doing all right, but I tell you we could do with a little of Noah's flood right now. All this heat and no rain is curing the grass off way ahead of time. If it doesn't let up we'll be feeding hay by late September, early October. And that will play hell on our supply. Could be we won't have enough to last through the winter. Norris thinks we ought to sell off five hundred head or so, but the market is doing poorly right now. I'd rather chance the weather than take a sure beating by selling off."

He sort of shrugged and closed his eyes. The whiskey was relaxing him. He said, "You're the boss."

"Yeah," I said. "Damn my luck."

I wandered out of the back of the house. Even though it was nearing seven o'clock of the evening it was still good and hot. Off in the distance, about a half a mile away, I could see the outline of the house I was building for Nora and myself. It was going to be a close thing to get it finished by our wedding day. Not having any riders to spare for the project, I'd imported a abuilding contractor from Galveston, sixty miles away. He'd arrived with a half dozen Mexican laborers and a few skilled masons and they'd set up a little tent city around the place. The contractor had gone back to Galveston to fetch some materials, leaving his Mexicans behind. I walked along idly, hoping he wouldn't forget that the job wasn't done. He had some of my money, but not near what he'd get when he finished the job.

Just then Ray Hays came hurrying across the back lot toward me. Ray was kind of a special case for me. The only problem with that was that he knew it and wasn't a bit above taking advantage of the situation. Once, a few years past, he'd saved my life by going against an evil man that he was working for at the time, an evil man who meant to have my life. In gratitude I'd given Ray a good job at the Half-Moon, letting him work directly under Ben, who was responsible for the horse herd. He was a good, steady man and a good man with a gun. He was also fair company. When he wasn't talking.

He came churning up to me, mopping his brow. He said, "Lordy, boss, it is—"

I said, "Hays, if you say it's hot I'm going to knock you down."

181

He gave me a look that was a mixture of astonishment and hurt. He said, "Why, whatever for?"

I said, "*Everybody* knows it's hot. Does every son of a bitch you run into have to make mention of the fact?"

His brow furrowed. "Well, I never thought of it that way. I 'spect you are right. Goin' down to look at yore house?"

I shook my head. "No. It makes me nervous to see how far they've got to go. I can't see any way it'll be ready on time."

He said, "Miss Nora ain't gonna like that."

I gave him a look. "I guess you felt forced to say that."

He looked down. "Well, maybe she won't mind."

I said, grimly, "The hell she won't. She'll think I did it a-purpose."

"Aw, she wouldn't."

"Naturally you know so much about it, Hays. Why don't you tell me a few other things about her."

"I was jest tryin' to lift yore spirits, boss."

I said, "You keep trying to lift my spirits and I'll put you on the haying crew."

He looked horrified. No real cowhand wanted any work he couldn't do from the back of his horse. Haying was a hot, hard, sweaty job done either afoot or from a wagon seat. We generally brought in contract Mexican labor to handle ours. But I'd been known in the past to discipline a cowhand by giving him a few days on the hay gang. Hays said, "Boss, now I never meant nothin'. I swear. You know me, my mouth gets to runnin' sometimes. I swear I'm gonna watch it."

I smiled. Hays always made me smile. He was so easily buffaloed. He had it soft at the Half-Moon and he knew it and didn't want to take any chances on losing a good thing.

I lit up a cigarillo and watched dusk settle in over the coastal plains. It wasn't but three miles to Matagorda Bay and it was quiet enough I felt like I could almost hear the waves breaking on the shore. Somewhere in the distance a mama cow bawled for her calf. The spring crop were near about weaned by now, but there were still a few mamas that wouldn't cut the apron strings. I stood there reflecting on how peaceful things had been of late. It suited me just fine. All I wanted was to get my house finished, marry Nora, and never handle another gun so long as I lived.

The peace and quiet were short-lived. Within twenty-four hours we'd had a return telegram from Jack Cole. It said:

YOUR LAND OCCUPIED BY TEN TO TWELVE MEN STOP CAN'T BE SURE WHAT THEY'RE DOING BECAUSE THEY RUN STRANGERS OFF STOP APPEAR TO HAVE A GOOD MANY CATTLE GATHERED STOP APPEAR TO BE FENCING STOP ALL I KNOW STOP

I read the telegram twice and then I said, "Why this is crazy as hell! That land wouldn't support fifty head of cattle."

We were all gathered in the big office. Even Dad was there, sitting in his rocking chair. I looked up at him. "What do you make of this, Howard?"

He shook his big, old head of white hair. "Beats the hell out of me, Justa. I can't figure it."

Ben said, "Well, I don't see where it has to be figured. I'll take five men and go down there and run them off. I don't care what they're doing. They ain't got no business on our land."

I said, "Take it easy, Ben. Aside from the fact you don't need to be getting into any more fights this year, I can't spare you or five men. The way this grass is drying up we've got to keep drifting those cattle."

Norris said, "No, Ben is right. We can't have such affairs going on with our property. But we'll handle it within the law. I'll simply take the train down there, hire a good lawyer and have the matter settled by the sheriff. Shouldn't take but a few days."

Well, there wasn't much I could say to that. We couldn't very well let people take advantage of us, but I still hated to be without Norris's services even for a few days. On matters other than the ranch he was the expert, and it didn't seem like there was a day went by that some financial question didn't come up that only he could answer. I said, "Are you sure you can spare yourself for a few days?"

He thought for a moment and then nodded. "I don't see why not. I've just moved most of our available cash into short-term municipal bonds in Galveston. The market is looking all right and everything appears fine at the bank. I can't think of anything that might come up."

I said, "All right. But you just keep this in mind. You are not a gun hand. You are not a fighter. I do not want you going anywhere near those people, whoever they are. You do it legal and let the sheriff handle the eviction. Is that understood?"

He kind of swelled up, resenting the implication that he couldn't handle himself. The biggest trouble I'd had through the years when trouble had come up had been keeping Norris out of it. Why he couldn't just be content to be a wagon load of brains was more than I could understand. He said, "Didn't you just hear me say I intended to go through a lawyer and the sheriff? Didn't I just say that?"

I said, "I wanted to be sure you heard yourself."

He said, "Nothing wrong with my hearing. Nor my approach to this matter. You seem to constantly be taken with the idea that I'm always looking for a fight. I think you've got the wrong brother. I use logic."

"Yeah?" I said. "You remember when that guy kicked you in the balls when they were holding guns on us? And then we chased them twenty miles and finally caught them?"

He looked away. "That has nothing to do with this."

"Yeah?" I said, enjoying myself. "And here's this guy, shot all to hell. And what was it you insisted on doing?"

Ben laughed, but Norris wouldn't say anything.

I said, "Didn't you insist on us standing him up so you could kick him in the balls? Didn't you?"

He sort of growled, "Oh, go to hell."

I said, "I just want to know where the logic was in that."

He said, "Right is right. I was simply paying him back in kind. It was the only thing his kind could understand."

I said, "That's my point. You just don't go down there and go to paying back a bunch of rough hombres in kind. Or any other currency for that matter."

That made him look over at Dad. He said, "Dad, will

you make him quit treating me like I was ten years old? He does it on purpose."

But he'd appealed to the wrong man. Dad just threw his hands in the air and said, "Don't come to me with your troubles. I'm just a boarder around here. You get your orders from Justa. You know that."

Of course he didn't like that. Norris had always been a strong hand for the right and wrong of a matter. In fact, he may have been one of the most stubborn men I'd ever met. But he didn't say anything, just gave me a look and muttered something about hoping a mess came up at the bank while he was gone and then see how much boss I was.

But he didn't mean nothing by it. Like most families, we fought amongst ourselves and, like most families, God help the outsider who tried to interfere with one of us.

A special offer for people who enjoy reading the best Westerns published today. If you enjoyed this book, subscribe now and get...

TWO FREE

A $5.90 VALUE—NO OBLIGATION

If you enjoyed this book and would like to read more of the very best Westerns being published today, you'll want to subscribe to True Value's Western Home Subscription Service. If you enjoyed the book you just read and want more of the most exciting, adventurous, action packed Westerns, subscribe now.

Each month the editors of True Value will select the 6 very best Westerns from America's leading publishers for special readers like you. You'll be able to preview these new titles as soon as they are published, FREE for ten days with no obligation.

TWO FREE BOOKS

When you subscribe, we'll send you your first month's shipment of the newest and best 6 Westerns for you to preview. With your first shipment, two of these books will be yours as our introductory gift to you absolutely FREE, regardless of what you decide to do. If you like them, as much as we think you will, keep all six books but pay for just 4 at the low subscriber rate of just $2.45 each. If you decide to return them, keep 2 of the titles as our gift. No obligation.

Special Subscriber Savings

When you become a True Value subscriber you'll save money several ways. First, all regular monthly selections will be billed at the low subscriber price of just $2.45 each. That's

WESTERNS!

at least a savings of $3.00 each month below the publishers price. Second, there is never any shipping, handling or other hidden charges—Free home delivery. What's more there is no minimum number of books you must buy, you may return any selection for full credit and you can cancel your subscription at any time. A TRUE VALUE!

Mail the coupon below

To start your subscription and receive 2 FREE WESTERNS, fill out the coupon below and mail it today. We'll send your first shipment which includes 2 FREE BOOKS as soon as we receive it.

LONGARM

Explore the exciting Old West with one of the men who made it wild!